Murder in ruins

The man was dead all right. His thr
surely not with the jagged flint clutcl
He lay on a stone slab in the ruins
priory.

That once hallowed place had rece
significance to a group of scholars
Traces of a hitherto unsuspected text,
ago, had revealed the burial there of t

The site was also the midnight mee
ists, whose nocturnal rituals include
orgies.

Perhaps the young man had been
the Earth Mother or to Satan, or
preserve the secrecy of the rituals?
more mundane reason, to do with the
have been the motive for his violent

The local CID, working day and
full, but the demons of darkness, bo
were eventually vanquished and cl
ousy and fear – were seen to comb
the ancient bards.

This fine, inventive first novel, wit
plot, combines with great expertise
demia with the elements of witch
workings of the CID. *Murder in ruins*

Richard Patrick Hunt was born ii
up and educated in Cambridge. He
and a company director and now li
Norfolk.

MURDER IN RUINS

Richard Hunt

Constable · London

First published in Great Britain 1991
by Constable & Company Ltd
3 The Lanchesters, 162 Fulham Palace Road
London W6 9ER
Copyright © 1991 Richard Patrick Hunt
ISBN 0 09 470480 5
The right of Richard Patrick Hunt to be
identified as the author of this Work has been
asserted by him in accordance with the
Copyright, Designs and Patents Act 1988
Set in Linotron 11pt Palatino by
CentraCet, Cambridge
Printed in Great Britain by
Redwood Press Ltd
Melksham, Wiltshire

A CIP catalogue record for this book
is available from the British Library

TO MY MOTHER

1

There was need for haste. Already the sounds of fighting could be heard, even through the solid oak of the church door, closed and barred as it was. Brother Ignatius shuddered slightly, as a shrill, high-pitched scream of agony was heard above the shouts and the clash of steel. 'Hold still, Brother,' the brown-cloaked figure of Brother James muttered, calmly, as he drew another breath. Ignatius swallowed hard and tried to concentrate. He looked at Brother James's face and felt some reassurance. He turned the cylinder a little further round, so that the light from the altar candles fell more directly upon the seam where the thick, round, lead plate was being sealed on the top of the heavy, grey drum. That had been the idea of Brother James. Considerable thought and prayer had been given to the problem of what to do with their treasures, in the event that circumstances might arise which would prevent their being taken to a place of safety. Prior William had even been heard to utter those words of doubtful sanctity, 'God will surely help those who try to help themselves.' Since then all had been prepared, and kept in instant readiness for the moment that they had prayed, repeatedly, should never arrive. Well, in spite of their earnest entreaties, that moment had come, and now it was the task of the three of them to put their plans into action.

The country was in turmoil, more so now than for the several years since the antagonism between King Stephen and his cousin, Matilda, had culminated in civil war and disorder. Roving bands of outlawed brigands were taking full advantage of the chaos in shires denuded of Sheriff and the disciplined forces of law and order, and had come from out of the forests, the fens and the wild moorlands, to plunder and pillage. Destruction and death had become commonplace. It was fortunate that the small patrol of King Stephen's men had sought shelter for the night. Their Captain, a veteran of many skirmishes, had set a guard, whose shrill, early warning of the raid had allowed some measure of resistance to be organized, else their throats might have been already cut. There was little chance of escape for the monks, although some of the soldiers might fight their way through the mass of the surrounding outlaws. Possibly the other small patrol, which had been expected, might yet arrive, even at this late hour, and put the assailants to flight, but that was all in the hands of a higher authority. In the meantime there was this patient work to be done. Brother James, the metalworker, had long ago made the cylinder of good, thick lead, which, together with the heavy round top plate, had been standing ready, out of the sight of prying eyes, behind the high altar. There, also, was kept a spare bronze blowpipe, with the thin lead wire and small jar of that special substance which Brother James needed to smear on the joints. All else then needed had been the small brazier and the charcoal, from the kitchen.

As Brother James blew down the pipe the tiny blue flame from the charcoal spluttered and roared, melting the lead wire into the narrow gap, sealing the top on to the cylinder. Provided the seals were done carefully the contents would remain safe and dry, indefinitely, so it seemed to them. Well and good: only then would they risk their beautiful codices.

The flickering flames of the altar candles threw strange, moving shadows on to the stone floor.

Outside, the shouting and noise drew much closer. Brother Ignatius looked up at the Prior's face, pale and drawn, and drew yet more comfort from his calm expression. Brother James put down the blowpipe.

'Father, it is done. I have sealed this as well as I am able. Thanks be to God,' he said, rising to his feet and brushing the dust from the front of his dark brown habit.

'You have done well, Brother James. Come now, let us put it into its place,' the Prior ordered, his voice deep and solemn, as befitted this sacred place. The cavity had been prepared many months ago. Although the three of them were now old and unused to labour, they rolled the heavy cylinder carefully into place and slid the even heavier stone coverings into position. Brother Ignatius, with his bare hands, spread dust into the gaps between the stones, rendering that area indistinguishable, even to the keenest eye, from any other part of the church floor.

Now there came a violent banging and hammering at the main door. Although it was barred and a wedge was placed in the iron latch to prevent its being raised, the door fitments were not strong enough to withstand any great amount of sustained force. Soon those outside would gain entry.

'Come, my sons,' Prior William said quietly. 'All is done as we have wished it to be. Now let us join together in prayer and ask God's blessing upon us and all our friends, and even on those who might wish us harm. Let us also ask him to give us of his strength in the times yet to come.'

The three monks knelt together at the oak rail in front of the altar, heads bowed low in final desperate prayers to avert the coming calamity. Prior William rose, laid a hand on each tonsured head, murmured a blessing and turned to face the door. In his right hand he extended the silver cross that hung from the fine silver chain round his neck. He looked up, momentarily, to the high timber roof trusses, and tears trickled down his cheeks as he faced the impending, senseless waste of all the past years' work in this Priory, the most dedicated labour in the scriptorium, making and illuminating copies of the Vulgate, their most venerable treasure. Still, they had done their best, the three of them, to preserve that. No one else knew, now, of its whereabouts. No other tongues could be tortured into disclosing its hiding place, not if the three of them kept silence.

As the door burst open to admit the yelling, ragged horde, the Prior rejoiced, knowing their own imminent deaths ensured that the secret would be kept. The screaming mob, maddened by the easy letting of blood, surged forward, killing the Prior, then striking with swords and knives at the two kneeling monks, snatching any object of value in their rampaging path. Flames from their torches ran up the wall hangings until the roof was well alight, and the dry timbers sparked and crackled.

The destruction complete, the mob withdrew, leaving only the dead and the dying in the wreckage. For although gravely wounded, Brother Ignatius was not dead. The thick oaken altar rail had thwarted a fatal blow and had also saved him later when the flaming roof beams came crashing down. It was thus that the King's patrol found him, next morning, the only living soul in the gutted, ruined priory. He mumbled incoherently while they tended his wounds and burns as best they could. Then they set him in a litter between two horses and took him the nearly twenty miles to the Abbey of Wherhampstead.

Brother Martin, the infirmarian, shook his head ruefully. 'His life hangs by the lightest of threads,' he told the Abbot. 'The wounds on his body I have cleansed and dressed with those salves that the Welsh monk from Shrewsbury gave me, and with God's help, they will heal, in the fullness of time. But the bone of his skull, here over the temple, is broken and I fear to touch it, lest I do more damage. It may knit together, but no skill of mine can heal the mind inside.'

'You have done all that you can, Brother Martin. The rest must be left to the mercy of God. We will include him in our prayers,' the Abbot replied.

After a few days it seemed that their prayers were heard, for Brother Ignatius's condition improved rapidly. Even though no words passed his lips he seemed to understand some of what was said to him. He could also walk a little way with short faltering steps, and so he was allowed to sit on a bench in the cloister where the afternoon sun would warm his bones.

However, the injured monk's mind was disturbed by one constant thought that troubled him. Then, as he wandered past an empty carrel in the scriptorium and gazed down at the familiar tools, he suddenly became aware of how he could fulfil the urgent demands in his mind. Here was the means. There was only one person to whom he could tell his secret. Sitting down, he spread a fresh vellum sheet on the wooden surface before him, setting the pot of black ink at one top corner and a water jar on the other, to stop it curling. Then he started to write.

'Your Holiness, I am Ignatius, a brother of Saint Matthew's, by Barnhamwell in England.'

He looked down at his words. The letters were ill formed. This surprised him, but his hand trembled as he watched it. He must go on. 'The greetings of William,

Prior. Our treasured codex is safe in the leaden box, tightly sealed.' The effort of concentration was causing his vision to blur. He closed his eyes for a moment. It took a great deal of effort, but he made himself go on. 'It is buried in the place prepared . . .' He could no longer hold up his head and it fell forward; the unhealed fracture struck the water jar. He died, instantaneously, and the water ran over the vellum, obliterating the painfully penned letters.

'He was trying to write something, obviously,' said the Abbot. 'Do all that should be done, as befits a member of our order. The vellum can be cleaned and used again.'

2

High up above, the smooth, bevelled, timber beams sectioned the high ceiling into neat, wide squares, the intersections being decorated with carved bosses of leaves and roses. The long walls of the Senior Common Room were panelled with highly figured, light brown oak; and from them portraits of dark-robed men stared haughtily down at those lounging in the deep leather chairs, grouped round a large, mock-Adam marble fireplace in which a few logs smouldered fitfully. The atmosphere of age in the room was contrived, for Downing College was new when compared with most of the colleges in the University of Cambridge.

'You can hardly raise objections now, George,' a dark-suited, bearded don said, ironically. 'The whole university has agreed to implement the scheme, and you can hardly say that our pathetic collection of manuscripts will present any special problems,' he continued, lazily reaching out to pick up his glass of port.

The lean features of George, the grey-haired Librarian, seated nearest the fire, showed exasperation. 'That's not what I mean at all,' he snapped, polishing the lenses of his spectacles furiously with a handkerchief. 'I admit that I shall not enjoy all the inconvenience of having to transcribe and reclassify all our important manuscripts, but I can fully appreciate the advantages of the new system for research when it is complete. What I am saying, and I had thought my remarks were clear enough for even the most simple of minds, is that if we must go to all this expense and trouble to put our manuscripts on to a computer, then at the same time we should copy them photographically as well, and in colour. Then researchers can have access to those copies, instead of the originals. As I said earlier, this will save much of the present handling. Then maybe we can preserve what we have – properly.' The Librarian leaned back in his chair and sipped his wine.

In the chair opposite him a short, plump, nearly bald man, whose vivid yellow velvet waistcoat seemed incongruous in such a setting, suddenly smiled and spoke.

'I understand what you are saying, George, but let me make a suggestion. You said "copy photographically"; I think you should consider using a video camera. That way, if I understand the process correctly, you will be able to use the same computer coding on video tapes. Researchers will then be able to work anywhere, provided they have access to a normal, domestic video unit.'

The Librarian drummed his fingers nervously on the brown-leather chair arm. 'Thank you, Edwin,' he said, after a few moments' silence. 'My initial reaction is that your suggestion would at least be a practical way of achieving the purpose I have taken such pains to spell out. That would be perfectly adequate, as far as I'm concerned.'

The previous speaker, Professor Edwin Hughes, smiled in smug self-satisfaction. 'Right, then. Are we all agreed on the expenditure for the equipment George needs? Yes? Excellent. Now, the timetable. The computers and other machines can all be installed and set up by early June. That's correct, isn't it, George?' After a slow nod from the Librarian, he continued. 'Then I suggest that the transcription should start during the summer, during the long vacation. Any objections? Good. I think we can drop the subject now.'

The Senior Common Room could now return to its usual somnolence, interrupted only by the occasional clink of a glass, a snore, or a low conversational murmur.

'What is all this reclassification for? Is it really worth all the effort?' asked Wendy Jacklin, one of Downing College's secretaries.

It was a scorching hot summer's day in the long vacation, but she still looked cool and composed in a red cotton skirt and white blouse. Her wavy brown hair was brushed back and hung down to just above her shoulders. Slim and attractive, with a ready smile, she was a popular girl, a couple of years or so younger than her companion, Jeremy Fry.

'Oh, yes! When it's all done, it will be marvellous,' Jeremy replied, before taking another bite from his sandwich. He was a tall, thin young man in his early twenties, fair-haired, bespectacled and still with a few adolescent spots. The heat of the day seemed to have affected him more than her, since his white cotton shirt stuck clammily to his back. Not only was it very hot, it was also very humid.

'All the major universities and libraries in Europe and America have agreed to classify their collections of old manuscripts, and put them on computer,' he told her. 'Of course it'll take years and years, but when it's finished all the computers will be linked. Then if you want to research something, all you'll need to do is to key in the right reference codes, and the computer will list out all the relevant existing manuscripts. The work of months will be done in minutes, and the computer will even provide a transcript of the manuscripts themselves.' He smiled again. 'Mind you, our lot are going to be one jump ahead with this colour videoing of the originals. I don't think many scholars are too happy to rely on someone else's translations – not completely, anyway.'

There was just a faint breeze of slightly cooler air moving over the sunlit grassy area of meadowland near a riverside pub called the 'Mill', where the two were having their lunch break. In places overhanging leafy willow branches shaded both land and water. Ducks squawked and splashed, or sat tamely in rows along the banks, keeping wary eyes open but welcoming contributions of food.

Wendy looked at Jeremy's enthusiastic face for a moment before saying anything more. They had only just met that morning: he to check the translations of the old manuscripts and reference-code them; she to enter them into the computer. There should have been another translator as well, but he had not turned up.

She knew that the project would take several weeks to complete, and that it was important that they should all get on well together. That was partly why she had accepted Jeremy's invitation to spend her lunch hour with him at this popular spot on the grassy banks of the river Cam.

'I didn't realize all this was on an international scale.

That accounts for all the fuss over the computer programs. It took quite a while to get them set up properly. My goodness, it's an enormous undertaking. How long have you been at university?' she inquired.

'I'm in my third year, or I will be next term,' Jeremy replied. 'I'm reading medieval history. That accounts for my being so dull and boring. That's how most other people see the period. I don't myself, of course.'

'I don't think you're dull. Do you care much for what other people think, then?' she said, gazing up at his face with large brown eyes. He wasn't bad looking, really, and was quite good company now that he was starting to relax a bit.

He grinned back at her. 'Only some people, the nice ones. The rest – well, I don't give two hoots what they think of me.'

'Good, that's just how it should be. Why have you stayed on for the vacation? Are you going to get away for a holiday at all?' she asked.

'Not this year. It's the money, I'm afraid. I can manage on my grant, just about, but there's nothing to spare. My mum and dad do their best, but I don't want to be more of a burden to them than I already am. Usually I take some job or other, fruit picking, that kind of thing. This year this cataloguing job came up. It's a bit of a "busman's holiday" for me really, studying those old manuscripts, but I like doing it, so I jumped at the chance. Besides, there are worse places than Cambridge to spend the summer.'

'That's true,' she murmured, thoughtfully, and changed the subject. 'What's that X-ray machine in the office to be used for, then? When I first saw it I thought it was a photocopier.'

He laughed. 'Yes, it does look like one, doesn't it?

That's been borrowed. It's specially designed for documents. Even if the lettering is faded or smudged, that particular machine reveals what was originally written. Ink soaks straight into the fibres of the parchment or paper, or whatever it's written on, so even though the ink might fade or even be erased, sufficient traces can be picked up by that machine. I'll show you how it works when we get back.' Linking his fingers together behind his head, he lay back, with a sigh of pleasure. 'Isn't this weather just glorious? I hope it lasts for the rest of the year. Are you a local girl, Wendy?'

'Local, born and bred. My father's one of the college porters, so you could say that I've been connected with the college all my life. You probably know my dad. He's the tall thin one, the one with the limp. He got wounded in the left thigh in Korea. Doesn't talk about it though,' she replied, tossing a crust to a duck that had been patiently waiting as she ate, and staring at her with a beady black eye.

'Wendy, this evening, would you . . .? I mean, how about coming out and having a pizza or a lasagna or something, with me? We could come down here afterwards for a walk or a drink,' Jeremy asked, nervously.

She hesitated for a moment.

'Yes, I'd like that. Thank you very much. Are you sure you can afford it, though? I can pay my own way you know,' she offered.

He smiled gratefully. 'Oh no, it's really nice of you to offer, but I would rather pay myself.'

'Suit yourself, then,' she replied. Then, turning to the duck, 'No. I haven't got any more, it's all gone, besides you look fat enough as it is.'

They wandered back to the college, talking contentedly.

*

Although it was as quiet as the adjacent College Library, the room in which Wendy and Jeremy were working had grey steel filing cabinets lining the walls instead of well-filled book shelves. It looked much more like a business office, which to a certain extent it was.

'I enjoyed that, Wendy,' Jeremy said, seated back at his desk.

'So did I,' she replied, contentedly, settling back at the computer and rechecking her previous entries. She could certainly input fast enough to keep two people coding and checking translations.

They worked on quietly, while birds chirped and squabbled in the ivy outside the window.

Jeremy got up with a document in his hand. 'Now here's where the X-ray machine comes into its own,' he said. 'A few words on this one are so faded they are almost unreadable. The previous translators have put in guesses, which are probably right, but with this machine, I can now make sure. Come and watch.'

He went over and switched on the machine, together with the attached video monitor.

'When the green light comes on, all I have to do is lay the document face down here and close the lid. We should see the writing come up on the screen in a moment. Yes, there we are. You see? I can make it clearer with the fine focus. That's better. See those smudged letters there? Quite readable now, aren't they? The experts guessed right. That's the Latin for northern boundaries.'

'What are these funny lines at the bottom?' Wendy asked, pointing to the screen.

'I don't know, I'll adjust the focus. It's writing, but I can't make head nor tail of it,' he replied.

'Perhaps it's on the other side of the sheet and upside down,' Wendy suggested.

'You could be right at that.'

Jeremy lifted the lid and turned the paper over.

'Now let's see. Well, well, well! What have we got here? *"Pontifex, nomen mihi est Ignatius."* That means the Pope, probably: "Your holiness, my name is Ignatius," that's what it says. It's not all that clear. I'll try to translate: "A Brother of Saint Matthew's near Barnhamwell, greetings (or respects, probably) from Prior William. Our (something or other) is safe, well sealed in a (something) box and buried in the place prepared" – and that's all. Well done, Wendy! You've found something that nobody knew existed. Now you can take a copy from this machine. Yes, we'll have three copies, two for me and one for the discoverer, as a souvenir. I'd better tell the Librarian about this,' he added, thoughtfully.

'He's not here this afternoon,' said the woman in the Bursar's office. 'If it's important, perhaps you ought to tell Professor Hughes. I know he's in his rooms because I saw him in the quadrangle when I came back from lunch.'

Jeremy found the rotund Professor in his rooms.

'Well, young man, this all sounds very exciting,' he said, after studying the copy, 'but I'd like to see the original. You'd better show me.'

They interrupted the conversation of a young man in jeans and an older man in a lightweight grey suit, who were talking to Wendy when they arrived back in the room by the Library.

'Hello, young Wendy. They've roped you in for this job, have they? Are you well?' the portly professor said, as he nodded a greeting to the other two and picked up the document in question.

'Vellum. This side is a transfer deed of land from one abbey to another, dated 1142. The other side has obviously been cleaned and must therefore presumably pre-date the writing of the transfer. Let's see it on the X-ray machine.'

Professor Hughes rubbed his chin, thoughtfully. 'A letter to the Pope, from Brother Ignatius of Barnhamwell Priory. I would hazard a guess that the first of those two words is treasured or venerated, this last one I think is lead something. Yes. Ignatius is saying that their treasured something is safely sealed in a lead box and buried in a prepared place. Since the letter is neither dated nor signed, it was obviously never sent and the vellum was cleaned and reused. The writing is shaky, but well formed; a sick man's, perhaps. Unlikely to be a drunken monk,' he observed, with a chuckle. 'Now, my friends, what do we know of Barnhamwell Priory? Let's look it up.'

Wendy and Jeremy followed him out into the main library.

'Abbeys and Priories, twelfth century; must have something, somewhere. What about this one?' He took down a thick, leather-bound volume. 'B – , B for Barnhamwell, or M for St Matthew's,' he muttered, turning the pages. 'At least it's in here. Established *circa* 1088. Produced several outstanding copies of the Vulgate Bible, only fragments of which now exist in the Bodleian. Pillaged and utterly destroyed in the year 1142. It was never re-established. Now that is very interesting, isn't it?' he said, drumming his fingers on the leather binding. 'You'd better classify it in the normal way for the computer, Jeremy, and see the Librarian with it in the morning. It will have to be added to our own catalogues, of course.' He smiled benevolently at the two youngsters, then pottered off jauntily, the copy of the ancient message still clutched in his hand.

It was early evening, and the blistering heat of the day had cooled to a pleasant warmth as Wendy and Jeremy walked down the tree-lined street from the house where Wendy lived with her father, towards the city.

'While you were getting ready, Wendy, your dad showed me his collection of old clocks and watches. He says that he even makes many of the parts he needs to restore them. He must be pretty clever to do that sort of thing.'

'Yes, it's been his hobby for years. He uses the small bedroom as a workshop. He's got a tiny lathe and things like that, but his eyesight's not as good as it was.'

'I thought we might try that Pizza Parlour in the Red Lion centre, if it's not too crowded and all right with you, Wendy,' Jeremy suggested.

'Yes, that sounds fine. Then we can wander down by the river afterwards. Do you realize that today is the longest day? It hardly seems possible that the year is half over already.'

A steaming, well buttered corn on the cob apiece, and a large ham and mushroom pizza between them, with a glass of cool white wine, satisfied even their healthy young appetites. Then, hand in hand, they strolled in the gathering dusk down to the river where they'd had their lunch.

The bridge was crowded with people, and noisy with laughter and the buzz of conversation. Someone was playing a guitar, singing and strumming a country-and-western number. A few young boys in bathing costumes climbed on the bridge parapet and dived, laughing, into the sparkling, dark water. At the pub bar it took a long while to get served with two iced lemonade shandies before they could squeeze themselves on to the bridge and find a place where they could lean over the parapet, to watch the boats, the ducks and the swimmers. The sun was very low in the sky, trees cast long shadows and the pub lights glowed brighter in the gathering twilight.

After a few moments Wendy asked, 'Jeremy, I've been thinking about that old manuscript we found this afternoon. Do you think it's possible that the lead box with the treasure in it could still be there? The book said that Barnhamwell Priory had never been re-established. Wouldn't it be wonderful if it was? You might even get a reward,' she said, her large eyes sparkling as she looked up at his face.

'That sounds like little Wendy Jacklin!' said a loud, slurred voice behind her. Startled, she turned to face a youth who had obviously already had more than enough to drink.

'Little Wendy Jacklin,' he repeated, staggering slightly, 'ready to roll on her back and open her legs for a bloody undergrad, huh! Us townies ain't good enough for you now, I suppose!'

His reddened face was thrust forward aggressively. Wendy instinctively tried to step back and Jeremy tightened his arm round her protectively. Suddenly the youth tossed the contents of his glass in Jeremy's face.

'Bastards, the lot of you!' he snarled, hurling the empty glass into the river as he staggered away muttering, 'Barnhamwell Priory. Bastards the lot of them.'

'Oh, Jeremy. I'm so sorry. Oh dear, your shirt's soaked.' Wendy looked anxiously up at him. Jeremy's eyes blazed.

'Not your fault,' he reassured her through clenched teeth. 'My shirt'll soon dry, although it might smell a bit. Come on, let's walk.'

'I'm sorry about that, Jeremy,' Wendy apologized. 'He's

a boy I went to school with. Martin Trent's his name. It's the old story about the town and gown. Some local boys do sneer at girls that have college boy-friends. I'm sorry that it happened to you.'

'He'd had a bit too much to drink. Let's forget it. I don't see why he should spoil our evening. It's a pity it's too late to hire a punt. On such a lovely night, it would be great to get up the river as far as Grantchester. The moon will come up soon, too.' Jeremy had recovered his good temper.

'Yes, it's a shame,' she said, but she was relieved all the same. She wasn't sure she liked Jeremy enough yet to risk punting up the river Cam to Grantchester with him in the moonlight; but of course she didn't say so.

3

An old Roman road runs just a little south of due east from Cambridge, up over the chalk hills. Daytime picnickers, walkers, hikers and evening lovers make up most of its present-day traffic. Thus it has degenerated into little more than a narrow, rutted track, running almost straight, for mile after mile, between stumpy, straggling green hedgerows and the occasional copse of birch, beech, ash or pine trees. Several of those undulating miles from the city the road climbs slowly up and over a long low hill. Here it has lost some of its protecting hedgerows, farmers having ploughed as close to the road as they could.

To the north, on this Midsummer's eve, the fields of ripening wheat shimmered like silver in the moonlight, and rustled gently, in the warm soft breeze. In the distance a clump of trees on a hill stood out darkly against a star-spangled sky. A lonely, lovely, deserted countryside, bathed in tranquil peace, and fragrant with the fresh scent of wild hedgerow flowers.

The faint, distant drone of approaching engines breached the silence, announcing the impending arrival of people, from several directions. They secreted their cars from chance eyes, in copses, behind hedges, and crept, silently, along the hedgerows and the sides of fields, converging on that lonely clump of trees. There was a protective barrier of brambles and nettles through which each person stepped with care, as they made their way to the secret open glade in the centre of the wood. Here was a softly grassed rectangular area, bounded by low ridges which were so well covered by grasses and ivy that only a very close scrutiny would identify them as the remains of walls. Towards the eastern end, the matted floor of turf and mosses was thin and dry, exposing areas of hard granite stone slabs, grey in the ghostly, silver light of the moon.

Those who had already arrived welcomed each newcomer with excited whispers, and there was a frequent inspection of watches, as though time in that half-forgotten place was now important. The last two shadowy pairs led, half dragged, half carried, a sleepy, drowsy girl, eleven or twelve years old. Whispered instructions were heard above the rustling of the leaves in the trees and places were cleared for candles on the walls. The young girl was made to drink from a flask that flashed silver in the moonlight. Then the group moved apart and removed their clothes, placing the neat bundles in dry places on the walls. The last man to arrive, now wearing only a white mitred head-dress bearing strange symbols in red and gold, called the others, who assembled on the grey stone floor, facing him. The naked slumbering child was laid on her back before him, her arms and legs outstretched. The group made a circle round her; even numbers, alternately man and woman, hand in hand, all completely naked. Sixteen bodies, some young and firm-fleshed, others gross and flabby.

Their ceremony commenced.

Invocations were sung. Strange-sounding chants filled the air, and the nocturnal wildlife fell silent, but many eyes watched, from the safety of dark places, the rhythmic, writhing contortions of the dancers.

After a while physical contact increased as breasts and sexually aroused parts were caressed and squeezed, sucked at or nuzzled. The candles illuminated faces that were now flushed, eyes that stared brightly, wildly and blindly. The dances became more frenzied, until it seemed as though that small area was a dynamic, vibrant world of its own, surrounded by a solid, impenetrable wall of blackness. A white cloth was cast over the sleeping girl's body and the leader flung himself down on her, his loins thrusting vigorously, but symbolically. One after another the males each repeated this ritual. The chants increased to a crescendo, then the circle burst into a wild-eyed, frenzied, screaming orgy of writhing, panting, coupling pairs. As exhaustion claimed the weakest, the stronger moved on to other, still active, partners. Gradually, panting voices grew quieter, until the last of the groaning, striving couples fell apart, and the gentle murmur of the breeze in the trees could be heard again.

Their passions assuaged, their rituals complete, they dressed their weary bodies and by ones and twos they retreated to their cars, away from that once sacred place; returning to their suburban homes and their respected roles in society.

*

The tall middle-aged woman looked tired and harassed; hardly surprising, Detective Sergeant Finch thought.

'Our plane was late, you see. We didn't get into Heathrow until twelve o'clock, Sergeant. By the time we'd got our luggage, gone through Customs, got the car from the car park, and driven home, it was nearly five o'clock, and then to find we'd been burgled – it was horrible.' She dabbed again at her eyes with a handkerchief. 'What a way to finish a lovely holiday! Everything had been so good up till then, and we spent so much money having the best burglar alarm installed, too. Yet they still got in.'

'You've left everything just as you found it?' Finch asked, sympathetically.

The woman nodded.

'Good, we'll need to take photographs and check for fingerprints, but that won't take long. Have you any idea yet what's missing?'

'My jewel box has gone, for one thing. I looked for that first. I didn't take much of it with me on holiday, I wish I had now, and my husband's collection of Coalport figurines has gone too, and all our silver. I know we're insured, but it's not the same, all our things were really nice. We'll never be able to replace them, and there's all the mess they've made. It's awful to think somebody has been through our things, handling everything. Oh, I feel so – violated!' She shuddered in disgust.

'I can understand how you feel,' Finch said, consolingly. 'It may be Dutch comfort for you, but I've seen places left in much worse states than this though. Sometimes they set out to spoil everything, as well as stealing things. It's interesting that they've left your video and television and your microwave; usually they're the first things to go. This lot must specialize. I'd like to wander round and make a few notes, if you don't mind.'

'Of course not.'

Tall, slim, and fair-haired, the grey-suited Detective Sergeant knelt carefully down to study the back door of the house. This was the exit door for the computerized alarm system that had heat and movement sensors in each of the other rooms of the house. To set it you tapped in the relevant secret code number on the wall-mounted control box, then had a minute or two to get outside and complete the circuits by locking the door. The bottom panel of the wooden door had been neatly cut away, leaving a hole big enough for even a large man to crawl through without difficulty.

Finch shrugged his shoulders, and turned his attention to the control box. Obviously it also had been tampered with, but the only sign was a hole, the size of a thumbnail, that had been cut through the metal, just above the row of buttons.

The bemused woman was still pottering in the hallway, as Finch went out.

'Do you think you'll be able to get any of our stuff back?' she asked, disconsolately.

'We'll do our very best, of course,' Finch replied.

Detective Chief Inspector Sidney Walsh pushed the window of his office wide open, letting the still fresh morning air drive out the overnight stuffiness.

Once a 'British Lions' rugby tourist, he was a little over six feet tall, ruggedly handsome, with shoulders a trifle too broad and a waist slightly too thick for him to be described as lean. His hair was more grey now than brown, betraying his age.

He smiled ruefully at Detective Sergeant Reginald Finch and Detective Constable Brenda Phipps, as he lowered himself back into his chair. Office work, on such a pleasant summer's day, was not the best thing to be doing.

'How did you get on with the burglary, Reg?' Walsh asked.

'It's almost identical to the one we had last week out at Waterbeach. Must be the same gang,' Finch replied.

'Have you heard from the equipment manufacturer as to how the intruder manages to switch the control box off?'

'Not yet . . .'

The telephone rang, interrupting him.

Walsh picked it up.

The Duty Sergeant coldly and bluntly informed him that there had just been a report of a body being discovered in an old, ruined church, a few miles from the city. The cause of death sounded particularly gruesome and definitely not accidental. Walsh and his team reacted quickly. They wanted to arrive at the site before the Forensic, 'Scene of the Crime' people.

'Where the devil are the ruins of Barnhamwell Priory, Reg?' the Chief Inspector asked, as they drove out of the police headquarters car park.

4

Walsh tried to drive fast but the congestion of the city traffic made that an impossibility; then, out in the countryside, it became necessary to slow right down, partly because the sun shone into his eyes, but also because the road narrowed and twisted its way up the low chalk ridges, known locally as the 'Gog Magog Hills'. (Gog being an ancient deity of a long forgotten people, and Magog, his consort.) Beech trees grew in a wood on the slopes, tall and strangely dark and gloomy on this bright summer morning. At the top of the hill he had to turn off the metalled road on to a wide trackway, before turning sharp left, on to the old Roman road itself. In places the ruts had worn deep into the dry, dusty flints of the subsurface and trees grew close, their branches intertwined overhead, making the leafy canopy of a witch's tunnel. Gorse and brambles narrowed the way and in spite of his attempts to keep the wheels of the car out of the deeper ruts, Walsh several times heard the ominous scrape of the underside on the rough surface of the central hump.

'I'm going to leave the exhaust behind if this goes on like this,' he muttered.

'I think you're nearly over the worst, boss,' said Reginald Finch at his side, moving hurriedly to avoid a long trailing, thorny bramble which had been turned aside by the windscreen and had come flicking in through the open window on the passenger side.

'You've been out here before then, Reg?' Walsh asked, knowing that Finch was a keen amateur archaeologist and quite often spent some of his spare time with his wife walking fields and tracks, armed with an Ordnance Survey map and compass.

'Plenty of times. This old priory ruin is on the left, about a couple of miles farther on yet. A few miles past that, away to the right is the old stone ring of Wandlebury, but that's on private land, so you can't just walk out there when you please,' he replied.

'This area was well populated in those days, was it, Reg?' asked Brenda Phipps, from the back seat.

'It would have supported a fair number of people, but there're two thousand years or more between Wandlebury and when the Priory was built.' He twisted in the front seat and grinned at the slim, pretty Detective Constable with the unruly, wavy brown hair. 'The light vegetation on these chalky hills could be easily cleared, you see, even with primitive tools. The grazing of cattle would also have helped to keep the land open, and not so far from here, there's the "Icknield way", running from Norfolk all the way to Wiltshire and beyond,' he told her, enthusiastically warming to his subject.

'Now look what you've done, Brenda,' Walsh interrupted, 'you've got him really going. Mind you, we may need some of your field craft out here, Reg,' he growled, more relaxed now that the condition of the track had improved. On either side of the road there was a rolling, swirling vista of yellowing corn, rippling in wind-blown waves.

Two men stood by the roadside on the next rising slope. As they drew closer, Walsh could see the top of a tractor over the low hedge on the right, and that of a car. He turned into the narrow entrance to the field and pulled up as close to the tractor as he could. There would be other vehicles following shortly. The car was an old, battered Morris Traveller; its number plate contained only three letters and three numerals. Leaning in the hedge was a police motor cycle.

Both men came over as Walsh got out of the car.

'Morning, sir,' the black-leather-suited constable said. Walsh smiled and nodded to him. Now that the throbbing of the car's engine had ceased, he could hear a skylark, high above his head. He stared upwards, but the sun was in his eyes, and he could see nothing.

'Is this the man that found the body?' Walsh asked.

'Yes, sir. This is Mr George Drew. He phoned the station. I was the nearest patrol, so they sent me here,' the constable replied.

'Tell us how you came to find it, please, Mr Drew,' Walsh asked the stockily built farm worker.

'I work on that farm over there.' Drew nodded vaguely northwards. 'It was this way, see. I come along this old track and I saw this car here, parked in the field. Well, that ain't nothing unusual, you might say, but I saw that someone's walked straight across that field.' He pointed over the road. 'You see, right through the growing corn. Look how it's trampled down,' he said, angrily. 'It ain't our land, but that's going too damn far, I said to myself. So I went off after him, didn't I? Over to that little wood on the hill there.'

'Did you go the same way as he did, through the field?' Walsh inquired, watching the man's face closely.

'Sure I did. The damage's been done, ain't it? Besides I wanted to catch him and give him a piece of my mind. Well, I found him all right, and I wished I hadn't, to tell the truth, 'cos he ain't a pretty sight, I can tell you.' He swallowed hard. 'It was all that blood. You'd think it wouldn't affect me like that, me being a farm worker and all. I wouldn't go back there when your man came. Not for all the tea in China, I wouldn't. I just showed him the way and let him get on with it.'

'So you followed through the corn as well, did you, constable?'

'Well, yes I did, sir, and it's as Mr Drew here says. The man's dead all right, his throat's been cut. I just looked, I didn't touch anything, or walk about more than I needed to, sir,' the constable replied, his face red and perspiring, even though he had undone the front of his leather jacket.

'I understand, but I don't want anyone else to go that way until the forensic boys have checked it. We'll have to walk round the side of the field, Reg.' He nodded at the constable. 'You and Mr Drew can stay here. Ask Mr Packstone from me, when he comes, to wait till I get back before sending his chaps over there,' Walsh instructed. The farm worker looked relieved and the motor-cyclist decided to remove his jacket. His blue shirt was dark with damp patches of sweat.

Walsh led the way on foot, back along the dusty Roman road, then through a gap in the hedge to the side of the field. 'We're not the first this way either,' he said, indicating with his finger a snapped bramble, still glistening with sap at the point of the break, and the long grasses, bent over by the passage of feet. 'Best keep on the field as much as you can. Be careful.'

He moved forward; the corn reached nearly up to his waist. Finch, slighter built but taller by an inch or so than Walsh, followed, carefully placing his feet on the softer soil of the furrows. At the edge of the wood there were indications of a passage forced through the surrounding brambles and an even clearer beaten track through a wide patch of nettles. A few waving fibres of white wool were hooked round a briar thorn.

'Don't disturb those, move round them carefully,' Walsh said quietly, stepping through the nettles. 'I reckon at least three people have come down this way recently, and in both directions. A man, a woman and a child. The child walked here, but I think, was carried back.' He did not stop to explain his remark, but instead carried on until he came to the low stone wall. Thick moss grew in places on the northern side and a tangled mass of creepers clung to the crevices. He swung himself over carefully but even so his trousers rubbed the mosses, leaving a green streak. He wished he'd been sensible like Brenda and worn jeans, but it was too late for that now. In the central glade it was cool and gloomy, compared with the bright sunshine outside. Then he saw the body, a young male, wearing faded blue jeans and a black cotton T-shirt, lying on its back on an area of stone slabs, cleared for the most part of grasses and moss. He swallowed hard. The throat had been crudely cut. The left arm lay outstretched but the right was bent up on to the chest and the hand clutched a jagged flint. Wide-open eyes stared blindly out from a face contorted with rage, or perhaps it was fear or pain. He heard the sharp, inward breaths of the two behind him, even though they were professionals, like himself. He stood still and looked round. He saw the stubs of candles, the turf trodden and scuffed. He'd seen enough for the time being, a nod of his head was all the other two needed. They followed him back to the road without uttering a single word.

There was a crowd waiting back at the car. Walsh beckoned a tall, grey-haired man. 'Hello, Richard,' he said. 'It's a nasty one. We've got to go in carefully.'

'It's definitely a murder then, is it?' asked Richard Packstone, head of the forensic department.

'It might be a ritual suicide, but we'd better treat it as murder for the moment. Come over here, you others, gather round,' he called. Picking up a small twig, he knelt on the ground and scratched a small rectangle in the dust.

'This is the ruin in that wood over there. The body lies there.' He pointed with the twig. 'This is the way we went in, along the edge of this field. That had been trodden within the past twelve hours or so by an adult male and female and a child, both ways, and maybe others, as well as the three of us. There're some wool fibres on the brambles just here. Another route in has been made straight through the cornfield. Mr Drew here and Contable Meadows have both been in and out that way. From what I could see there are ways in from the other side as well. Right, got that?' He stood up, brushing the dust from his knees.

'There would appear to have been some sort of ritual in there last night. The grass in the middle could have been trodden down by upwards of a dozen or so people. The style of the death could be sacrificial. What is quite clear, though, is that you chaps must first start on the outside and work your way into the ruin. There are footprints in the dust and plenty of thorny brambles to scratch the unwary, so you might even find blood samples. I want an accurate description of each and every one who has gone in and out of there during the past twenty-four hours. Smith? There you are. Well, you're going to have to be everywhere at the same time. I want photos every step of the way. Right, Richard, I'll leave you to organize your chaps. It might be better if you concentrated on the route through the corn, it's the shortest, then we can get at the ruin without treading all over the evidence.' He tossed the twig to one side and moved away, leaving Packstone to direct his men.

Smith came over.

'I've brought the new video cameras, sir. I thought we'd try them out, as well as still photos,' he said, slipping yet another strap over his crew-cut head.

'Good idea, I'll leave all that to you. Meadows, have you found out who owns this Morris yet?' he asked the motor-cycling constable.

'Yes, sir. It's registered in the name of Martin Trent, at an address in Collaridge Road. They've looked up his driving licence number, he's aged twenty-one last month. It could be the man in the ruin, sir,' Meadows replied.

'You could be right. Have you got that map, Reg? Good, open it out on the bonnet. This lane here, and this one as well, both of them might give access to the other side of the wood. Reg, get the Station on the radio, have them send someone out to close those lanes. We don't want the public wandering about, and while you're on to them, get them to send out the portable loo thing, and something to eat and drink. It's going to be a long day. Now, Brenda, where's the nearest farmhouse? There's one, on the map, there, and another here and here. Take my car, go and talk to them, they might have seen or heard something last night.'

He felt in his pocket for his pipe. The old dottle fell out as he gently tapped it on his heel. Had he covered all aspects for the time being? Already Packstone's teams had moved off. He walked over the road. Two men had started in the corn; side by side, on hands and knees, they each meticulously searched the ground before them within two light aluminium frames, each exactly a yard square. Then they moved the frames forward one yard. Smith stepped between them, to photograph the new area. The kneeling men leaned forward again to study the dry clumpy soil. It would take an hour or so, at that slow pace, to reach the little wood on the low hill which surrounded the ruins of the ancient priory. Even so, Walsh was content. That meticulous searching, as painstaking as any archaeological dig, should miss nothing.

'If you find any flint arrowheads, axes, bits of pottery or such like, keep them for Reg Finch,' he called, cheerfully. The men turned their heads and grinned back at him.

The police doctor came over. 'I've got a flask of coffee. Fancy a lukewarm cup, Sidney?' he asked. Walsh's eyes lit up.

'That's a great idea, Fred. Yes, please. We've got a bit of waiting to do, I'm afraid.'

'No matter, it's a lovely day and it's nice to get out in the fresh air. What's it like over there? They tell me it's an old ruin.' He pointed towards the distant hill.

'It's dank and gloomy under the trees and all overgrown. There's very little left of the walls. It's not easy to visualize it as a priory chapel, it's more like an ancient sacrificial grove. That reminds me, I'd better get something moving on strange religious cults. Thanks for the coffee. You must be an ex-Boy Scout, carrying that flask, being prepared!' Walsh grinned at him.

He called headquarters on the radio phone. 'I want you to search the records. I want to know everything and anything we've got on file concerning strange religious cults. Satanists, that sort of thing. Yes, I know it'll be a long job. Yes, ask around, delve, use your head.'

The light breeze felt cool on his neck. There was a gentle buzzing of bees in the hedgerow. That skylark was working overtime today. The sun shone down, warm, refreshing, comfortable. Walsh settled down to wait.

5

The sun had risen past its meridian and now its light bathed the eastern end of the ruined church through the high canopy of leafy branches. The forensic team had worked its way through the cornfield, inch by inch, and had picked over and photographed the trampled, grassy area within the walls.

Walsh leaned forward to hear the conversation between Packstone and the doctor.

'You're quite right, Richard. The left hand is not as bloodstained as it ought to be if it was suicide, and that flint was never used to cut his throat. It was something much thinner and sharper than that, but not, I think, a knife,' the doctor said. 'The edges of the cut are too ragged for that. A slash from right to left, and there's a sign of dirt on the flesh at the beginning of the cut. I can't tell you offhand what was used; I might have a better idea when I've got him on the table. We'll see. There's this gash on the back of his right hand, too. Possibly he raised that hand to ward off the blow. I think we can turn him on his side now! That'll do. It looks as though he's had a bash on the side of his head here.' He pointed to an area just behind the right ear. 'Aged about twenty, I'd say. Been dead a little over twelve hours: since, say, between one and two o'clock this morning. Recent dental work, there's a new filling in the upper left canine tooth, and the plaque has been removed. That should facilitate identification, if all else fails. I suspect that we'll find a high level of alcohol in what blood there is left in him. That's about all I can say at the moment, Sidney. I doubt that the autopsy will tell us much more, to be honest. Anyway, I'll send in my report, in the usual way.'

'Thanks, Fred. Are you saying that he bled to death when his throat was cut? He wasn't killed by the blow on the head?' Walsh asked.

'Oh no. The blow certainly didn't kill him. His heart was still pumping away, that's why he bled so much. No doubt about that.'

'This is interesting, Sidney,' Packstone remarked. 'Look here, you see these marks on the edges of these stone slabs, as though something's been forced between them. A spade, perhaps. Now you come to look at it, you can see the dirt in the crevice round the edges has been disturbed, loosened just a bit, as though the stone had been raised a millimetre or so on this side. He was lying on it, so we couldn't see it before. There's another thing, Sidney. These slabs, they've not been cleared recently; several years ago, I would guess from the grass in the gaps. Maybe it's not important. The rest of the area hasn't been disturbed for centuries. It rather looks as though some cult might have used it regularly for their weird rites. This poor fellow might be an offering to the Earth

Mother or a sacrifice to Satan, but that doesn't explain the flint knife being in his own hand. I don't suppose he had any suspicion of the role he was going to play when he turned up here last night. It constantly amazes me the strange ideas people still have in this day and age, calling on devils and the like.' Packstone shook his head.

'There's plenty of people believe in that sort of thing. People you'd think would know better, too. Look at all those that play with the Ouija boards and have their palms read. Not as bad as this, thank goodness, but they all believe in supernatural powers of some sort,' the doctor added.

'Well, I wish they wouldn't do so in my patch,' Walsh said emphatically. 'We can have the body moved now, can't we?' he asked. 'Then if your chaps have had their lunches, they can get back on the job.'

Finch and Brenda stood to one side of the group, listening and watching. They followed the others back through the cornfield. Both seemed lost in their own thoughts and content to be so. The time did not seem to be right to engage in the discussion of theories and motives; not yet, not until their minds had absorbed all the available information and sifted it into some kind of order. They watched as the body was carried on a stretcher to the waiting ambulance and driven away along the dusty track, followed shortly by the doctor in his grey, Peugeot hatchback. Packstone roused his drowsy teams from their break, setting them to complete the examination of the other access routes and the rest of the wood.

'It's a pity there's no direct proof of identity at the moment,' Packstone said later. 'Although I should think it's pretty certain he's the owner of this car. I've got just about everyone out here now; hopefully we'll be finished by five or six o'clock, then it'll be just lab work.'

'That's good, Richard. I'm anxious to be able to poke around in the wood,' Walsh replied.

'I suppose you are, but don't worry, we're getting plenty of data. I'll be able to give you a full-scale map showing which individuals went where and where from,' Packstone said confidently.

'I hope you can, but I'd still like to see things for myself. For instance, there's a shoe print, just inside the wall, that I think is the victim's, coming in, but it's superimposed on a woman's print that looks as though it's going out. I'm by no means convinced that things are quite as simple as they seem. We'll see,' Walsh replied, philosophically.

Packstone looked at him thoughtfully. 'I'll get back there and get the wood finished as quickly as we can. See you later.' He gave Walsh a curious glance as he strode away.

'Now you've got him worried, boss. I reckon you've got aboriginal blood in you somewhere. I've seen you at it before. You can leave them all standing at tracking and woodcraft,' Reg Finch remarked.

'It's purely observation, Reg, but it's a pity there's so little opportunity for that sort of thing,' Walsh replied, regretfully.

'HQ have just rung through, Chief. One of Smith's photos of the dead man has been taken round to the house in Collaridge Road. Martin Trent's mother says it is him all right. They're going to take her up to the mortuary for a confirmatory identification. So now we know for certain,' Brenda informed him.

'Go and comb your hair, girl,' he growled. 'You look as though you've been dragged through a hedge backwards.'

'That's not far off being true, Chief,' she replied, unabashed.

'Well? How did you get on with those farmers you went to visit?' Walsh asked.

'No joy, I'm afraid. I saw the three of them. Mrs Nestor, that's the wife at the farm south of here, she heard a car in the early hours, when she had to get up for a pee, but she's no idea what the time was. The other two, that's a Mr Privet in the farm to the north-east, you can't see it from here but it's behind those far trees over there, and Mr Manton – the chap who found the body works for him – both heard nothing suspicious. They all say that farmers are early to bed and early to rise, besides which there are dog walkers and courting couples use these tracks and lanes at all hours. They'd never have any peace if they worried about all the cars they heard at night,' Brenda said.

'I suppose so. Pity, though. Well, never mind. Which one farms these fields round the wood?'

'That's all Mr Privet's land! Well, not exactly his, he's a tenant farmer.'

Later, back within the mossy wall of the ruin, Packstone looked hot and dishevelled. 'I think we've done quite well, really,' he said, running a dirty hand over his red, sweaty brow and through his grey hair. 'We've identified at least fourteen individuals, maybe sixteen. It looks as if they may have stripped and left their clothes in separate piles, down there, at the west end. That's where we found these things,' he said, pointing to several clear plastic bags lying on the ground.

'There're a few coins, a hair grip, a cigarette lighter, several paper tissues, cigarette ends, a couple of empty lager cans and the *"pièce de résistance"*, this dentist's appointment card.' He handed it to Walsh, a white square of cardboard.

Walsh read it out loud. '"Dolmen & Dunne, Drewest St, Cambridge, Dental Surgeons, 9 a.m. July 18th." Well, at least that's something to go on. What else have you got?'

'Well, these are all the items of recent origin. We've also got a whole bag of other things obviously here much longer than the last twenty-four hours. We'll check them through again in the lab, but I don't think they're relevant to this case,' Packstone replied.

Walsh bent down and riffled through the larger of the bags, revealing a rusty penknife, bottle tops, old pennies, even a battered golf ball.

He looked up at Packstone. 'You've finished the wood completely now, have you?' he asked.

'Yes. We're working the field edges to the west and north now. There are markers to show where each item was found. Smith's been over it all at least once, but he's gone to get some more video cassettes. He wants to walk the whole lot again but in the reverse direction,' Packstone told him.

'Good for him. Right, you two, I want to circle the edge of the wood and follow each line of entry up to the walls here. Then we'll walk the inside of the wood, crossing our own tracks. We'll do this area last. Come on.'

With a slightly amused expression Packstone watched the trio set off. He shook his head, then turned away and went out of the wood to supervise his own teams. Walsh had noticed that look, which he'd seen before, but it didn't worry him.

Packstone was in charge of the 'Scene of the Crime' teams, many of them civilian specialists, trained to observe the minute traces left by humans before employing the latest scientific means to analyse and catalogue them. Then, one day, those traces would be used to prove a suspect's guilt, or innocence. It wasn't that Walsh distrusted Packstone's team; on the contrary, he held them in the highest respect; he just liked to see things for himself. Besides, detection was his responsibility. So the three of them repeated the search procedure themselves, and spent the next two or three hours crawling through the brambles and grasses, meticulously following each of the now well-trodden ways into the centre of the wood. Then they circled within the wood until they were again back inside the low walls, all equally dirty and dishevelled.

The sun was low in the sky when they met Smith there, sitting on the wall making adjustments to his video camera. 'The light's just about gone, sir,' he said, reluctantly. 'But I've nearly finished. There's a hell of a lot of ground to cover in a place like this. Still, I've got it all here. With these cassettes you'll be able to sit in comfort in front of your TV and go over it all again whenever you like and as often as you like,' he said, enthusiastically patting a grey canvas haversack that was slung over his shoulder.

The three of them worked their way round the walls, parting the long blades of grass, until Walsh expressed himself satisfied. Then they walked the long hedgerows to the west and north in the growing twilight. It was getting quite dark by the time they got back to the car. Many of the others had gone, but Packstone was still there, loading plastic bags into the boot of his car.

'You'd better have these as well, Richard,' Walsh said, handing him three polythene-wrapped objects. 'There's a packet of cigarettes, a handkerchief and a black ink Bic pen. Probably out of the pockets of your team!'

Packstone's face reddened. 'I'll wring some people's necks when I get back!' he growled. 'A job on this scale is bad enough without your own lot dropping their stuff all over the countryside. Thanks, Sidney; here, mark on this plan where you found them. We might just have missed them.'

Walsh laughed, and clapped him lightly on the

shoulder. 'Don't let it worry you, Richard. You've done a damned good job today.'

Packstone grinned. 'Can't stand here yapping. I've still got lots to do. See you later.'

They followed the rear lights of his car up the road, back to headquarters.

Walsh's first job was to brief a crowd of reporters. 'The deceased was Martin Trent, a young local man, in his early twenties. His mother has confirmed his identity and he lived in Collaridge Road. At the moment we are treating the death as suspicious. The body was found in an old ruin, some miles out of town. You all know where, but I don't want it in the papers tomorrow. We need to go over the ground again and I don't want hordes of sightseers. Can I have your word on that?'

He looked round. A few heads nodded. 'Right! That's all I can tell you at the moment. Please don't go and harass the Trent family, they are very distressed, as you can imagine,' he ended, with little hope that his request would be respected.

After a wash and a cup of coffee Walsh went upstairs to see the Chief Constable.

The big, bluff, red-faced man behind the desk wasted little time on formalities, although he hadn't seen Walsh for several days.

'Come in, Sidney, and sit down. Now, what's all this I hear about a body in an old ruined priory?'

Walsh sat down and absent-mindedly rubbed his left ear, which was slightly distorted from a scrummage incident, years before.

'Yes, the body of a youth was found this morning out at Barnhamwell. There had obviously been some sort of Satanic ritual out there last night, about twelve or fourteen people, we think. The manner of death makes it look like a sacrificial killing, although it is just possible it could have been a drug-induced suicide. It might have been part of the ritual, but at the moment I'm not sure it was either. My feeling is the lad arrived after the ritual was over and the people gone, because beneath his body there were traces that suggest a spade had been used in an effort to move one of the stone flags. It's not much, I know, but I think the lad might have been doing that when he was attacked. Then someone set it up to look like a ritual killing. We'll see. We've got a few leads. That's about all I can tell you at the moment. We'll know more tomorrow when Packstone's worked through his stuff. It's made more complicated because people habitually tramp along the edges of fields, and a lot of what his chaps picked up has been lying around for donkey's years,' Walsh explained.

'I see. Well, you seem to know what you're about. Come and see me tomorrow when you know more. Keep me up to date, Sidney.'

6

'Poor Martin was a good boy, really he was. He was never any trouble. I can't understand why anyone should want to do him any harm, honestly I can't,' Mrs Trent said tearfully, her eyes reddened and her plump face pale and drawn from weeping. Her sturdy, red-haired husband put his broad hand over hers.

'He was never in any trouble, never mixed with the wrong sort of people, and he was doing very well at his work too; they were pleased with him. He was passing his exams and tests at evening classes at the Tech. He was a trainee welder with that engineering company off Newmarket Road, you see. He'd been there since he left school. He really enjoyed it. It seems such a stupid waste,' he said, bitterly.

Walsh nodded sympathetically. 'Do you have any idea where he was going when he went out last night? Was he going to meet any of his friends, for instance?' he suggested, quietly.

'Well, I don't, not really. He would have been at the Tech if it wasn't for the holidays. I should think he went round looking for his mates. He'd got lots of chums, but none in particular, if you know what I mean,' Mr Trent told him.

'Did they have a regular meeting place, do you know?'

'I don't think so. It would be one of the pubs in town if they had, I suppose, there are plenty. Maybe he went round several of them, I don't really know. It wasn't that long ago when there was a whole gang of them but they've got girl-friends now, that's what broke them up. Martin had a girl too, very struck on her he was, until he found she was also going out with a chap from one of the colleges. That really upset him, he wouldn't have any more to do with her, even though she came round one evening to try to make it up; but that was several weeks ago. I suppose he's been a bit at a loss since then, it's understandable, and there have been a few times recently when he'd had a bit too much to drink. But we all have to go through that sort of thing, finding out what our limit is, don't we? I didn't make too much of it. He'd have got over it.'

'Did he or any of his friends have anything to do with mystical rituals, Satanism, Druids, reading the cards, that sort of thing?' Walsh asked.

'Good heavens, no! I've never heard him talk about anything like that. He'd have called people like that a load of nutters. Hold on a minute, now I come to think about it, I'm not so sure he didn't come back sometime during yesterday evening,' the father added, rubbing his chin thoughtfully.

'What makes you say that?' asked Walsh.

'Well, he'd got one of these metal detector things. They'd had a bit of a craze on them a year or so ago, but it died down soon enough, when they never found anything valuable. Anyway, I know it was lying on the bench in the garage yesterday when I came home from work, because I saw it, but it wasn't there this morning; and I think a spade's gone as well,' Mr Trent added.

'That could be helpful, but there was nothing like that in his car when we found it. Any idea what time he might have come back, then? It could be important.'

'I don't know for certain that he did take them. Anyone could have nicked them because the garage doors don't lock. We were in bed by eleven, so it would have been after then, I should think.'

Walsh rubbed the side of his nose. 'You mean you'd have heard him if he actually came into the house? In that case he may have just pulled up outside, gone into the garage to get his detector and a spade, and then driven off. You didn't hear a car stop outside?' he asked.

Mr Trent shook his head. 'No, I can't say that we did, but it's quite a busy road. You get used to the sounds of cars, and don't take any notice of them.'

'Perhaps you'd write me out a list of Martin's friends, all that you can think of. No, not right now. I'll get someone to call round for it first thing in the morning, if that's all right with you? Maybe one of them might know something. Well, thank you for helping me, particularly under the circumstances. If you think of anything else or if there is anything that I can do for you, please let me know, won't you?' Walsh said, getting up to leave.

'You just get the bastard that did it, Inspector. That's the best thing you can do for us now,' Mrs Trent cried tearfully.

Walsh drove home in a very thoughtful mood. It seemed fairly certain that young Trent hadn't been directly involved in any strange rituals: consequently, if he had been made a sacrificial victim, then it had been by chance, just because he was there, at that remote spot. Possibly he'd been caught spying on the ceremony and had been killed to preserve the secrecy of the rituals, but that didn't explain his presence there in the first place, or the absence of the metal detector and a spade from his father's garage. Maybe Trent hadn't taken the metal detector. Wasn't it more likely that he'd taken a girl out there for romantic, moonlit lovemaking? Possibly he might then have become curious about the activity in the wood: in which case, who and where was the girl?

He had no answer to those questions; not tonight, anyway.

The next morning Walsh sent Reginald Finch to Dolmen & Dunne, the dentists, to find out who had appointments for nine o'clock on July 18th. Brenda Phipps's task was to organize a small team to question those people named on the list of Martin Trent's friends, as well as seeking information on Satanistic societies from the vicars and clergy in the city's churches. It was after they had both left, while he was clearing a few other case files, that the telephone rang. The operator told him that Professor Hughes of Downing College would appreciate a word, if he wasn't too busy. Walsh rubbed his nose. He had met the professor before, on another case, and had found him a very shrewd man indeed. If Hughes wanted to talk to him, it would be about something important, of that he had no doubt. He told the switchboard to put him through.

'Good morning, Inspector. Now I know you're a busy man, so I'll come straight to the point. I've read in this morning's newspaper of the death of a young man whose body was found in a deserted ruin. Now, was that place the ruined Priory of St Matthew at Barnhamwell? I do have good reasons for asking,' the professor added.

'Yes, Professor, it was, and the young man's name was Martin Trent,' Walsh replied promptly.

'Oh dear! I was afraid it might be. In which case I have some information that might be of assistance to you, and there are a couple of young people here with me who saw him the evening that he died. Are you busy? Of course you are. What I mean is, shall we come over to you or you to us?'

'I'll come to you, Professor. I'll be with you in about fifteen minutes,' Walsh replied.

'That's fine.'

Walsh grabbed his jacket from the back of his chair and hurried out. It wasn't far to Downing College, it was within walking distance, across a large, grassed, open area known as Parker's Piece; no need to use his car.

Hughes was waiting for Walsh at the open door, and ushered him into a suite of large, comfortably furnished rooms with mullioned and leaded windows overlooking a sunny quadrangle.

'Inspector, I'd like you to meet Miss Wendy Jacklin, one of our secretaries, and Jeremy Fry, who is one of our students,' Hughes said.

Walsh nodded to them both and smiled.

'Now let's all sit down. Wendy, would you pour out the coffee, please?' He waited until they were all seated. 'Let me tell you the story, Inspector, then you can ask what ever questions you want.'

Walsh smiled again. He wanted information but it was better to let the professor tell his story in his own way, and quicker too, probably.

'Wendy and Jeremy are engaged on a project to transfer the text of all our old manuscripts on to a computer system, and reclassify them. The words on one of the documents were faded and almost illegible. When Jeremy used an X-ray machine to clarify them, he discovered traces of a hitherto unsuspected text. One that had been erased many centuries ago.' He handed Walsh a sheet of paper and then continued his story. 'That is a translation of what he found, Inspector.'

Walsh blinked, wondering what the connection was with the death of Martin Trent, until he noticed the word Barnhamwell. Then he read it carefully.

'Interesting,' he commented, dubiously.

'Yes, it is, isn't it? A text well worth some consideration. Well, these young people discussed their discovery; down on the bridge over the river by the old Mill, on the night this young man Trent died. Their conversation could well have been overheard by Trent, who had walked up and was standing behind them. That's the story, Inspector. There is a little more, but that is best told by them, in their own way.' The professor smiled reassuringly at the girl, whose slender fingers were twisting nervously in her lap.

'What can you add to this story then, Wendy?' Walsh asked kindly.

She looked up at his face. 'Jeremy had asked me out for a meal, and afterwards we went down to the Mill for a drink. It's nice down there in the evenings, usually. We were leaning on the wall looking down at the boats and the river, just talking. Martin and I went to the same school, and he must have come up behind me. I think he had been drinking, because he said some rude things to me and threw his drink over Jeremy. There was no provocation at all, honestly. We weren't interested in anyone else,' she said, in a clear precise voice.

Walsh nodded. A couple of young lovers out on a mild summer's evening would have little interest in other people.

'Can you remember just what you both were talking about? I presume it was to do with this?' He raised the copy of the document in his hand.

'Yes! I'm afraid it was. I can't remember my exact words, but I know I mentioned Barnhamwell and whether Jeremy would possibly get a reward if the treasure was still there.' She turned her head to look at Jeremy, who nodded in confirmation.

'What was it that Trent actually said to you, Wendy?' Walsh asked.

She looked embarrassed and Jeremy spoke for her. 'He called her a tramp because she was with me, an undergraduate. He said that the town boys were obviously not good enough for her any more and that we were both bastards. He'd definitely had too much to drink, because he staggered as he went off muttering to himself; but I do remember, he definitely mentioned Barnhamwell, so he must have been listening. Another thing, if he hadn't been, he wouldn't have known that I was in college; not many of us stay here during the long vacation.'

'Was he alone?' Walsh asked, starting to fill his pipe.

'I didn't see anyone with him as he went off. I don't know where he was going, but he headed back up Mill Lane, towards Trumpington Road,' Jeremy replied.

'And what time would that have been?'

'I should think it was about quarter to ten, or thereabouts. Wouldn't you, Wendy?'

She nodded. 'Then we walked along by the river, towards Newnham.'

'And Jeremy took you home later, Wendy, did he? Was that late?' Walsh inquired.

'Oh no. I was home about eleven. Yes, Jeremy walked home with me,' she replied.

Walsh lit his pipe. He'd got something, now, that connected Trent with the old ruins and might also account for the metal detector, but it also opened up a whole new avenue for enquiry.

'Just when did this lost text of yours turn up, Professor?' Walsh asked, when his pipe was burning satisfactorily.

'I wondered when you would ask that, Inspector,' Hughes remarked shrewdly. 'In the early afternoon of the day before yesterday.'

'So the knowledge of its existence would have been confined to relatively few people at the time of Trent's death,' he said, thinking out loud. 'Trent knew, and the three of you. Who else?'

'John Rochester was there when Professor Hughes came to look at the original on the X-ray machine, Inspector,' volunteered Jeremy. 'He's the other chap working with me doing the translations and reclassification. He should have started with me that morning, but he'd been delayed travelling back. He'd just popped in to explain, but he heard about it. Besides, I showed him the original when the Professor had gone,' he admitted.

'And the man from the computer bureau was there as well, Jeremy,' Wendy added. 'He'd only come in to make sure everything was all right with the equipment, but I'm afraid he knew as well.'

'What's his name, Wendy?' Walsh asked, while writing in his notebook.

'Roger Tomkins. We get our printer ribbons, discs and things from the Computer Centre in Change Street,' Wendy told him, but she was biting her lip and looking distressed. 'And, well, I did mention it to my dad,

Inspector. That was before Jeremy came round. Oh dear! I do seem to have caused so much trouble talking about that wretched treasure. If I hadn't said anything Martin Trent wouldn't have overheard me, and he wouldn't have got killed. I'm so sorry, I didn't mean any harm.' She blinked back tears, but seemed comforted when Jeremy took her hand in his.

'I don't think you have any cause to reproach yourself, Wendy,' the Professor said quietly. 'I myself also mentioned the matter to the Librarian, after dinner that same evening.'

'I'd like Wendy and Jeremy to make official written statements. You could do that down at the station this afternoon,' Walsh said, looking at his watch. 'It won't take very long. Come about half past two, if that's all right with you, Professor.'

After the two youngsters had left, Walsh shook hands with the plump, cheerful professor.

'By the way,' Walsh asked, as he left the room, 'do you know of any strange cults, here, around Cambridge? Satanists, Druids, that sort of thing?'

'So that's what was going on in the old priory, was it? I thought it must have been something like that. I can't say that I've heard of anything in recent years, but I'll sound out a few people if you like. You think that this young man Trent might have gone out there to look for this treasure of Brother Ignatius, and disturbed a Satanist ritual, do you?' Professor Hughes asked.

'On the face of it, that's a possibility, but I have a feeling that it's probably a bit more complicated than that. We shall see. Thanks again for your help,' Walsh replied.

7

'I know who it is, boss, it's this Mrs Haverston. She was the only one who couldn't produce her dental appointment card.' Reginald Finch sat on a chair by the far side of Walsh's desk. His long fingers turned a page of his notebook. 'She's a schoolteacher, divorced, and lives on her own in a flat out at Girton. Aged about forty, I'd say. She denied having anything to do with any strange cults, but she was lying; no doubt about it. You could tell from her face when I told her why I was making enquiries. She said she was at home that evening, on her own, then she clammed up.'

'Right, good work, Reg. Get someone working on it. Talk to the neighbours, the headmaster of her school. You know the sort of thing. Then come back here. I've found a link between Barnhamwell and Trent, Brenda's taking statements at the moment. Then we can compare notes and plough through Packstone's preliminary report, together,' Walsh suggested.

'I've done better than that, boss. I've already put a tail on Mrs Haverston. I phoned through and called young Pinder out. I waited outside her flat until he'd arrived. I know he hasn't been on plain clothes duty long, but he ought to be able to handle it all right. Be good experience for him. I can't see her going long without having to talk to someone about my going round there. It's a pity we couldn't tap her phone,' Finch told him.

'Sorry, Reg.' Walsh grinned broadly. 'I can't imagine what I was thinking of, telling you how to suck eggs.' The slightest frown appeared on his forehead and he wondered why he'd said that. It wasn't the kind of thing most Detective Chief Inspectors would have said to a Detective Sergeant. But there, he didn't give a damn about maintaining the haughtiness of his position and liked those who worked closely with him to feel relaxed and comfortable. They worked better that way. That was probably why he got called 'Boss', or 'Chief' or 'Captain', instead of the formal 'Sir'. He'd never had any problem with insubordination because of it. He shrugged his shoulders as Brenda came into the room with the typed statements of Wendy Jacklin and Jeremy Fry.

'Good, now you're here we can go through Packstone's report together.' He picked up the phone, and dialled a number. 'Richard, have you got just a few minutes to talk us through the maps and diagrams with your report, please? It'll save us a bit of time. Thanks.'

Walsh put down the telephone.

'He's coming up. It looks as though there were as many as eighteen or twenty there, all told, at some stage or other. This suggestion that two sets of tracks might be those of people who left with the others and then returned later is important, so is the fact that one of them was a woman. I've got an uneasy feeling that Trent might have had someone with him.'

Brenda looked up at him in surprise. 'Now why do you say that, Chief?' she asked.

'It's hard to put an impression into words. Try to picture Trent's mental state and attitude of mind when he met those two down at the Mill bridge. Probably he was already feeling morose. Assume that he hadn't met any of his mates and didn't like drinking on his own, particularly among a crowd of people who were thoroughly enjoying themselves. Given his likely mood under those circumstances, you can understand his aggressive behaviour when he saw his old school girl-friend with an undergraduate. What puzzles me is what happened then, to get him treasure hunting in the middle of the night. If he'd had a few more drinks, got into a fight and tossed a brick through a window before going home to sleep it off, that I could understand. There's no logical connection unless someone else is involved, possibly someone to whom he boasted about knowing where a treasure was buried. Maybe he was then persuaded, in his befuddled state, to go out and find it, there and then, instead of waiting until the next day, like any sensible person would.' Walsh rubbed his chin.

Brenda didn't look convinced. 'Has anyone else been reported missing, Chief?' she asked.

'Yes, but not anyone likely to be concerned with Trent. I'll be told as soon as any more "missing" reports come in.'

Packstone came into Walsh's office.

'The problem is that so many people are wearing these trainer shoes nowadays. For instance, these prints here, here and here' – he pointed – 'are all the same, in every respect, as the shoes Trent was wearing. He could have made three separate visits to the site, all from different directions, but it's unlikely. Alternatively, there were three different men, coincidentally with identical shoes,' Packstone explained.

'What about the stride patterns, are they all similar?' Finch asked.

Packstone shook his head, ruefully. 'We've looked into that, but the ground was so uneven that there's no consistent pattern, not in the softer areas where the prints were found. That goes for all the prints, of course. We've made estimates of the weight and height of each of the individuals, but the weight is probably the more accurate. It was Trent that went through the cornfield, that's definite, closely followed by someone else, lighter and with smaller feet. Those two moved round the ruin a little way and spent some time kneeling behind a bush, here, near the west corner. They're very faint, but you can just make out the knee marks. That's on photograph 12/38. That would have been before the main crowd left, because there're some overprints on photo 12/47. Now here's the confusing bit; apparently the same pair of shoes came in from the north, as well, and crouched down here.' Again Packstone pointed to the spot marked on the drawing spread out on the desk.

'Where's the other set of tracks, Mr Packstone?' Brenda asked.

'They come and go along by this hedgerow here, but the last set of tracks out this way have the same print as Trent's. They go out along here, and preceding them is the same person who followed Trent in through the cornfield.' Packstone stood up as he finished speaking.

'So if we were to say that Trent, and possibly a girl, walked in this way through the cornfield, saw the ritual going on and hid behind the bushes until it was over and the Satanists had left. Then they went in with a spade and a metal detector. Mr X, who had also been hiding, at this point here, comes in and kills Trent. Then he goes off, taking the girl with him. That would fit all the facts, Richard, wouldn't it?' Walsh asked.

'By and large, yes.'

'Could you tell from the prints whether the girl, assuming it was a girl, went willingly, or if she was being forced, Mr Packstone?' Brenda inquired, looking up at the tall man.

'We did discuss that question, but bearing in mind that the prints were made in the middle of the night and the roughness of the ground, we didn't think that we could make a positive judgement. It's possible, though,' admitted Packstone.

'You were right then, boss. Trent did have someone with him,' Finch remarked.

Walsh started to fill his pipe. 'Are there any girl's names on that list Trent's parents gave us, Brenda, the one of all his friends that he might have met up with? A stranger would hardly have gone off with him at that time of night.'

Brenda flicked through the pages in the file. 'No, Chief, they're all men's names. Constable Wrighton is out interviewing them at the moment. Do you want me to go to see his parents and get the names of any girls he knew?'

'Would you mind?' Walsh asked.

Brenda smiled, and went out.

'Have you found out much about strange religious sects, Sidney?' Richard Packstone enquired.

'Not a great deal, yet. There's certainly plenty of evidence of activity in the area, although most of the local clergy think that it's not as bad as it used to be. Traces have been found in several remote, ruined or disused churches, at various times during the past few years. On one or two occasions there has been evidence that a sacrifice had been made, usually chickens, but never human traces.

'Unfortunately, names never come with the information. We've got a few chaps out visiting the fortune-tellers and the known mystics. We might find out something that way. From what I've heard the Satanists are out of the normal run, and go too far for most people's comfort. Satanism seems to frighten the tarot card readers, white witches and Druids,' Walsh remarked.

'I think it's something to do with a fear of powerful mystic forces that makes people want to keep on the right side of them. Keep the evil ones happy, then you should be all right. Do it well, and you might even get rewarded,' Packstone muttered, half to himself.

'Unfortunately the workings of the mind are not visible. These people lead normal lives and look just like everyone else. There's no way you can pick them out of the crowd,' Walsh said.

He and Finch worked their way through the rest of the report after Packstone had returned to his laboratory.

'Frankly, Reg, I don't see that we can do much more with all this. It's too early to have another go at your schoolteacher, we've got to wait until young Pinder reports in. We've set it all up for tonight's questioning at the Mill, and the city pubs. So I think it'd be best if you go and see that computer fellow and that other young undergraduate that's working with Jeremy Fry. Find out what they were up to the night before last. Then I think we've covered all the obvious lines of inquiry, until something else breaks.'

That was what he found himself telling the Chief Constable, some ten minutes later.

'Sorry, Sidney,' the CC had said on the phone. 'I've got to go down to London tonight and I wanted to see you before I go. So you'll have to come up now.'

'Prime suspects at this stage must be the people that attended this ritual,' Walsh explained, 'but as I say, I'm worried about the possibility of there being another missing person. I've sent Brenda to find out about his girlfriends. If one of those has gone missing I'll pull out all the stops, and I'll release a photo to the press, if that's all right with you?'

'Of course. Do whatever you think necessary, Sidney. I'll be in London all day tomorrow, and won't be back until late the day after. My secretary's got the number, if you need to contact me.' The Chief Constable looked at his watch and started to gather some papers together.

Walsh went back to his office, where he settled down to work, until Brenda phoned through. 'I've got the names of some of the girls Trent knew, Chief. I thought I'd check on the one that he was going out with until recently, Joanna Silvers, the one that had been dating an undergraduate. I've been round to where she lives, but there's no one there. The neighbours say that the mother and father are away on holiday. Joanna didn't go with them, but they haven't seen her for several days. I've rung the personnel office where she works, but she hasn't been in for two days, Chief. I'm going on to see the other girls on this list. She might be staying with a friend and taking time off work, her attendance record at the firm isn't good. Um, on the other hand, no, I won't, Chief. I'll come straight back first. I've got a photograph of Martin and Joanna from Mrs Trent. If I hurry, there'll be just time to get it blown up and then we can give copies to the team that's going round the pubs and places tonight.'

'Yes, you come back with the photo, Brenda, but read out to me the other names on your list. I'll get the patrol cars on to it, it'll be quicker.' He wrote rapidly. After she had rung off, Walsh rang the Duty Sergeant and read out the list of names and addresses.

'And if the girls are there, ask them if they've seen Joanna Silvers, or know where she might be. Make sure that they know we are worried about her safety, otherwise they might clam up, thinking they might get her deeper into trouble. Get the cars on it without delay, and let me have their reports as soon as you can.' Walsh put the phone down and drummed the fingers of his right hand on the desk. 'I rather think we've found out who our missing person is,' he said to himself, 'and I don't like it one little bit.'

8

'John, Edward, Rochester, and you're twenty-two,' said Finch, writing in his notebook. 'Where's your home address?'

'25, Manor Road, Sheffield.'

'Born in March then, that makes you a Pisces. The way Neptune's situated, it should be a good week for you,' Finch suggested.

'That's a load of crap. I'd rather be out enjoying myself than stuck in college, working.'

'Oh well, never mind,' Finch continued, 'I understand you were present when Professor Hughes was discussing the discovery of a previously unknown text with Jeremy Fry.' He paused to observe an affirmative nod. The young man sitting opposite him looked a little nervous, but no more so than was to be expected in an interview with a policeman concerned with a murder inquiry.

'Did you agree with their translation?' Finch asked with a smile.

Rochester looked surprised at the question. 'Well, yes, I did, I suppose. It's the interpretation of the meaning that might be questionable.'

'In what way?'

'Well, you've got to remember that its writer was a monk. "Treasured" to him wouldn't necessarily mean "valuable", in its materialistic sense.'

'True,' agreed Finch. 'What do you think the message refers to, then?'

'Probably relics, so-called saints' bones, a piece of the true cross, some nonsense like that. Professor Hughes thinks it might refer to their sixth-century Irish copy of St Jerome's Vulgate. He might be right, such a thing might have acquired an aura of veneration and be rated with holy relics.' Rochester shrugged his shoulders. 'We'll never know.'

'Oh! So you don't think there's anything left to find in the old priory, then?'

'What? After eight hundred years, buried in the ground? Fat chance,' Rochester sneered sarcastically.

It was Finch's turn to shrug his shoulders. 'So you weren't tempted to go out there that evening, with a spade, and have a look, then?' Finch asked, looking directly at the young man's face.

Rochester's eyes glinted aggressively. 'No, and I didn't murder anyone either.'

'Did you tell anyone else about it?'

'No, I didn't think it that interesting,' he replied, impassively.

'Well, what did you get up to, that evening?'

'Not a lot. I had dinner in college, of course, then wandered round town for a while. Went to bed about elevenish, I suppose. I was pretty tired, you see. I hadn't slept much the night before.'

Finch's raised eyebrows effectively asked why.

'I'd been home with my parents for a few days. My mum said I could borrow her Mini while she and dad were on holiday, but it broke down on the A1, when I was driving back to Cambridge. The clutch cylinder packed up. So I spent most of the night in a lay-by. I couldn't get it fixed until next morning. That's why I couldn't start transcribing those manuscripts with Jeremy Fry until the following day,' Rochester explained.

'Your mum's car's a Mini, you say. What's the colour and registration?'

'It's yellow. BVF297Z.'

'And where do you park it?'

'In the road, outside my digs, if I can.'

'Did you wear those trainers the night you got back? Size nine, aren't they?' Finch asked, pointing down at Rochester's shoes.

'Probably, yes, I must have done, and you're right; I take a nine.'

'You say you wandered round the town that evening. Did you meet anyone you knew, or have a drink in a pub, or anything like that?'

'I was on my own for most of the time, but I met a couple of girls in the Wimpy, and got chatting to them. They weren't bad, but the one I really fancied saw a friend go by outside and went off after him. The other one stayed with me and was friendly enough.'

'Do you remember their names?'

'The one that went off was Jo, and the other was Mandy. She'd got a boy-friend already, she said, but we had a bit of kiss and cuddle anyway when I took her home. I didn't ask her surname, we weren't that serious, if you know what I mean.'

'Come in, gentlemen, come in.' Professor Edwin Hughes greeted his visitors, and ushered them into his rooms in the college.

'You both know George, our Librarian, don't you? George, you know Arthur and James, from King's College, I'm sure. Good of you both to come over. Sit down, would you like coffee or sherry?'

'Sherry, Edwin, please. I like this little water-colour you've got here,' Arthur said, looking up at the small painting hanging on the wall. 'Very nice. Thanks,' he continued, taking a sparkling crystal glass from Hughes and sitting down in one of the high-backed, leather armchairs. 'Now, what's all this about that old priory, Edwin? You didn't say much on the phone.'

Hughes moved one of the highly polished little tables nearer Arthur's chair, before he sat down. 'It's quite interesting really. It concerns King's because the Priory's on your land. I'll tell you about it. We've started re-cataloguing our manuscripts for this computer exercise. One of them is an old deed transferring land to Wherhampstead Abbey, dated 1142. It was put on the X-ray machine and turned up a bit of text that we didn't know about. It had obviously been cleaned off the vellum before it was used for this land transfer agreement. Here are some copies, see for yourselves what it says. The Priory was destroyed in 1142 according to our Chalmer's reference book.'

Arthur took the paper and read it carefully.

'I've looked up what we have on the Priory at Barnhamwell. There's a reference in the chronicles of the Augustines of Huntingdon about it. Unruly elements of Matilda's forces, while Stephen was besieging her in Oxford Castle, ravaged the area, burned the priory and slaughtered the monks. There was only one survivor, and he died of his wounds after a few days. This could be his writing. Interesting, though; it looks as though they were prepared for trouble and hid their valuables in time. This Ignatius must have written it down to tell those at Wherhampstead where to find it, although he addresses his letter to the Pope. Wherhampstead Abbey certainly took the opportunity to lay claim to the Priory lands for themselves, that's really why it was never re-established.'

'Yes, but you notice that Ignatius doesn't in fact say where the valuables were put, other than that they were buried "in the place prepared". In addition to that, I have these other copies to show you. As you alter the focus of the X-ray machine you can see the different depths of ink penetration, obviously more intense under the pen's point. You see that last one, the ink has spread nearly all over the paper. It looks as if something was spilled over the vellum before the ink was dry. In fact that might be why the writing stopped abruptly,' Hughes remarked.

'It's certainly very interesting. The codex must have been their Vulgate Bible. They seem to have specialized in making copies of that. Interesting, but I don't see how it affects us. This detective work is fascinating, Hughes, but I don't see that it adds much to our knowledge,' Arthur replied, laying the copies on the table by his chair and picking up his glass again.

Hughes rose to refill it.

'But don't you see? The writing is clearly that of a sick man, possibly even a dying man, and if the spillage occurred before the ink was dry it would have been illegible,' he said, in a somewhat impatient voice.

'Oh come, come, Edwin! Are you trying to suggest that because of the spillage the message wasn't passed on? You can't possibly believe that this lead box is still there. It's over eight hundred years ago,' the King's College don said scornfully.

'The chances are small, of course, but there is still a possibility. Consider the proposition, "tightly sealed in a lead box". I am given to understand that if the lead was pure enough and properly sealed, its contents could have survived that period of time, provided the conditions in which it was buried were stable. Of course we don't know, but you must agree that it is a possibility. In addition, Ignatius doesn't say where it is and I doubt whether Prior William would have allowed many people to know his plans. So, what I am saying is that it is possible that the box wasn't recovered, and that it is possible that it hasn't decomposed. As to that, even if it has, they may well have put other things that would have survived in the box, their reliquary caskets, their objects of precious metals. Now do you see?'

'Yes, Edwin, I do understand what you are saying. I would agree that the chances of finding anything are minimal. That said, though, any chance of finding a genuine Vulgate must be worth the effort. What do you want us to do, Edwin?' Arthur asked.

'I think we should organize a search. In fact, a proper archaeological dig. As the owners of the land on which the site is situated, obviously you are the best ones to organize it, although we, here, do have an interest and will be quite ready to assist. The ground was obviously sanctified at some time. I suggest that we obtain the consent of both the Catholic and the Church of England authorities, as well as the department for ancient buildings. I can organize all that, if you are in agreement. Then we need an archaeologist to take overall charge of the excavation itself, but I don't see a problem. There's Tynan of Jesus College, for instance – he's still here, since his dig in Syria fell through, and there are others whom we could use. Are we agreed, gentlemen? A joint venture between both our colleges. Good, I'll start getting the consents arranged – we might even be able to start before next term begins, but I do suggest we keep the knowledge of what we are doing to as few people as possible. If word were to get out the site would be invaded by hordes of treasure hunters, and that would ruin everything. The chances are that the harvest will be in before we start, too, so I don't see that we even need to tell the farmer until we are ready to begin. It can't affect him at all,' Hughes suggested, wondering if there was any way he could get that codex to end up in his own college's library, if it did indeed still exist. Very unlikely, but worth pondering.

*

'You were at Downing College in the afternoon of the day before yesterday, I believe, Mr Tomkins,' Finch asked, his pale blue eyes looking round at the tiny bench, with soldering iron and pin vice, and the shelves of equipment in the little office. Most of it was for computers, but there were other things as well, burglar alarm control boxes, sensors and car phones. On the wall hung a framed certificate stating that one Roger Tomkins was an associate of the Institute of Electronic Engineering and Design.

'That's right. I believe I was,' replied the neatly dressed man, who was probably in his middle thirties. 'I'd just popped in to see if they had got everything they needed. They've just started a new project, you see.'

Finch nodded. 'They had a little bit of excitement while you were there, I understand.'

'You mean they'd found something written on one of their old parchments that they hadn't known about before? Yes, that's right. Mind you, they were using pretty sophisticated equipment. Very specialized, a document X-ray machine. A very limited market for a thing like that, no real commercial potential for the likes of us. We carry a wide enough range of stuff as it is.'

'Do you remember what it was they found?'

'Oh yes. It was something an old monk had written, about putting their valuables in a safe place. A priory at Barnhamwell, if I remember correctly. That stuck in my mind, because I've lived round here all my life, and I didn't even know there was a priory at Barnhamwell. Mind you, it's a tiny enough little place,' Tomkins replied.

'Were you interested enough to go and have a look for yourself?'

'I'll be honest, it did cross my mind. But by the time I'd finished here and we'd taken the kids to the fair on Midsummer Common, it was much too late for that sort of thing. It was getting dark, you see.'

'So you went home from here, and then to the fair. Did you go out again after that?'

'I did, as a matter of fact. It was such a nice evening, so I popped down to the local while the wife put the kids to bed.'

'What time did you get back home from there?'

'I don't know for sure – midnight, or a little after.'

'You drove, presumably? What car do you drive?'

'Yes, I took the car. It's a grey Rover 213. F279 ZXY.'

'Which is your local?'

'I use the Groom and Horses in Trumpington.'

Finch nodded, and looked up from writing in his notebook. 'You must have changed. You wouldn't have gone to the fair in a suit, surely?' he asked.

Tomkins looked surprised. 'Of course I changed. Jeans and trainers, that's my usual gear for mucking about at home.'

'Trainers. You look a size nine?'

Tomkins nodded.

'Your birthday's in August, isn't it? That makes you a Leo, I shouldn't wonder. The way Neptune's situated you should be having a good week.'

'Should I? I hope you're right. I'm not into that sort of thing.'

'Come on now, Mrs Haverston, it really would be far better for you to tell us everything,' Walsh said to the tight-lipped, nervous woman sitting opposite him at the interview room table. 'We are preparing a warrant to search your flat, and then we will be interviewing both Miss Carpenter and Mrs Houndell, as well. So we are going to learn all about it eventually, but that way everyone will know what we're up to. The press are very good at ferreting things out, too. Imagine! All your friends and neighbours will learn about your goings on. It'd be much better if you told us willingly, you know. That young man, Trent, was murdered, and in a particularly unpleasant way too. Forget what you see on the television about the police. This is for real, there's no more serious crime in this country than murder, even if they have done away with the death penalty. Besides, it's your duty to give us all the help you can. We know you were one of those people who held a pagan ceremony in the ruined priory at Barnhamwell. We have no reason to believe that you, personally, are responsible for the young man's death, but we must find out who else was there, and what you all might have seen, in order to find the real killer. You do see that, don't you?'

Walsh spoke quietly, but emphatically. The woman was resentful and stubborn; she was also very frightened, but he was fairly certain that she would clam up altogether, if he started banging the table. Mrs Haverston stayed silent, but her bottom lip was caught between her teeth and a muscle near the corner of her left eye was twitching. Suddenly she looked up at Walsh's face.

'If it was just up to me, I'd tell you, but it isn't. It's up to our, er, leader,' she pleaded.

'Well, ring him up and ask him. You can tell him that we're bound to get all the names eventually, and it'll be far better if he co-operates. Here, you can use this phone. It dials straight out,' he said, pushing the grey telephone across the table. 'I'll go and see if I can get some coffee made for us. You'd like one, wouldn't you?'

She nodded. 'Yes, please,' she replied, watching him as he got up and went out.

'Organize a couple of cups of coffee for me, will you please, John?' Walsh asked the Duty Sergeant.

'Yes, of course, sir. Is she talking?'

'She will, but I've done most of the talking so far, Sergeant, that's why I need those cups of coffee.'

'Yes, sir. I'll organize them straight away.'

Walsh gave Mrs Haverston another couple of minutes before he went back in. She was still talking.

'Yes, I'll do that then. If he agrees. Hold on a minute, he's just come back in. I'll ask him.' She looked up at Walsh. 'He says that we have nothing to be ashamed of, and he insists that our privacy be respected, but I can tell you all the names, provided you agree that we needn't be interviewed here, in the police station, and that no uniformed people will come to visit us at our homes. Please, it's not much to ask, is it?' She waited, anxiously.

'I'll agree to that,' Walsh replied generously.

'It's all right, he agrees.' She spoke into the phone, much relieved. 'I've been in such a state since they came round this morning, I can tell you. I said to Jill this morning, "It makes your skin creep, to think of people asking questions about you." "It's not fair," she said, but I told her, "They're going to pry and pry, until they get what they want." Oh, he's rung off. Well I can tell you all about it now, Inspector. There doesn't seem a lot of point in me going home first, and you coming out to see me, does there? So I might as well tell you here.'

'That's right, Mrs Haverston, we can have our coffee in peace. You can give me the names of all those people that were there with you, then you can tell me all about what happened in that old priory, on midsummer eve.'

'In the mood she was in, Jo would've done anything to get Martin back, miss,' Mandy Street remarked tearfully.

'How could that be? I thought they'd busted up weeks ago, that's what his parents said,' Brenda Phipps asked.

'So they did, but they'd been friends for years, you see, and going steady for ages.'

'I don't see. Why did they bust up then? It seems to me it upset Martin more than Jo.'

'Well, Jo met this undergrad from Jesus College. He was smashing, a big hunky chap. He said he'd like to take her to the May Ball, so you can understand, can't you, miss? Get taken to a May Ball? Well, any girl would, wouldn't they? But he was only leading her on. You know what he was after, and when he'd had it he didn't want her no more. "I ain't half been a twit, still you lives and learns," she says to me. That's when she tried to get back with Martin.'

'Martin's parents said she'd been round to see him, but that he wouldn't have anything to do with her.'

'Yes, but that didn't stop her. "He'll come round when I can get him on his own," she said, and she'd have done it, too. I told her she should go out with someone else, to make him jealous – there were plenty who fancied Jo. Bill Smart, for instance, he's been after her for years. But she said no, it wouldn't work with Martin. Oh God! What could have happened to her, miss? Will she be all right?' Mandy asked, anxiously.

'We'll have to see. Now, you and Jo went to the Wimpy that night. Did you go there often?'

'Not specially. My boy-friend, Bob, was away on a course with his firm, so I was on my own, you see, and Jo said at work as how she was bored, not having anyone to go out with. So I said we could go out together. Better than sitting at home moping, anyway. She was getting on all right with that chap John too, until Martin went past the window, then she was off after him, like a shot.'

'So you got left with John Rochester?' Brenda prompted.

'Yes; I was afraid someone might see me with him and tell Bob, so I said I was going home. He said his car was round the corner, and he'd take me if I liked. He seemed nice enough, so I didn't mind when he parked round the corner from my house, by the allotments. It was a bit early to go in really, so I let him kiss me and that sort of thing. It was fine to start off with, but all of a sudden he got real randy, miss, and he got into a hell of a bloody temper when I tried to stop him.'

'This was in a Mini?' Brenda asked, her eyebrows raised in surprise.

'No, of course not, he'd got me on the grass verge by then, the bastard, trying to get me jeans off. He'd got me arms behind me back, and he slapped me real hard when I screamed, but he heard someone coming and I managed to get free and run home. I heard him drive off like a maniac,' Mandy said, angrily. 'The bugger would have raped me.'

'Did you see the person he heard coming?' Brenda wanted to know.

Mandy shook her head. 'I didn't hang about, I can tell you.'

'Which way did he go then, when he drove off?' Brenda asked, her face serious.

'Towards Fulborn. He's a menace, that John what's-his-name, and bloody dangerous too.'

9

'Mr Nestor?' Walsh inquired of the tall man that came to the farmhouse front door.

'That's right! What can I do for you?' he asked, smiling pleasantly.

'I'm Detective Chief Inspector Walsh, and I'd like to

have a word with you about that bit of trouble we've got, at the old priory.' Walsh waved his arm vaguely in the direction of the horizon to the north.

'Terrible thing that! Come on in.' He led the way through the hall into a large kitchen, and introduced the cheerful, plump woman there as Mrs Nestor and the two youngsters, still eating breakfast at the broad oak table, as his children.

'Nasty business, Inspector,' Mrs Nestor commented as she placed a cup of coffee on the table in front of Walsh. 'It makes you wonder what things are coming to. Mind you, I never did like that place much. Dark and gloomy in those woods, though it's pretty sometimes, when the bluebells are out. I've told the children to keep well away from it. It's a worry, during the holidays, you can't keep your eye on them all the time. Roll on term time, again, I say.' She grinned affectionately at her two offspring.

'One of your Detective Constables has already been round asking if we saw anything that night, Inspector,' Mr Nestor remarked.

Walsh nodded, and felt in his pocket for his pipe and tobacco pouch.

'Do you mind if I smoke?' he asked, his brown eyes looking up at Mrs Nestor's homely face.

She shook her head.

'It's not on your land, I know, but it's been used by a strange religious sect for their summer solstice ceremony, probably not for the first time, either. I was wondering what you might know about such things, locally, I mean,' Walsh said, teasing the tobacco into finer shreds in the palm of his left hand before gently packing it into the bowl of his pipe.

'We've only been here ten years, Inspector. Not as long as Mr Privet or old Mr Manton, but I suppose you'll be going to see both of them,' Mr Nestor suggested.

'Old Mr Manton's your best bet. He's been in that farm all his life, and knows everyone round here. Mr Privet might know something, but he's more involved with his bowls and church-wardening,' Mrs Nestor interrupted.

'That may be so,' her husband continued, 'but in fact there's more goings on at the Wandlebury Ring, you know. That's to the south-east of here. It's the Druids they have problems with there, year after year, even if it is an ancient monument. But I vaguely remember something to do with that old priory, that was when we first came here, but I can't for the life of me think just what that was.' He shook his head regretfully.

'That place is a damned nuisance,' Mr Privet said, in his strangely hesitant way. 'It's marked on the Ordnance Survey maps. "Site of priory", it says. So every Tom and Dick of an amateur archaeologist thinks he's got a right to go and have a look, even though there's nothing left to see. I used to think of it as hallowed ground, something rather special, but I gave up trying to keep people away, years ago. Waste of time. I wanted to fence it round once, but the College's agent said no, I mustn't. So I don't bother with it any more. Why should I? I've over six hundred acres. I'd need a small army to stop people trespassing.'

'Have you had any problems with people with metal detectors recently?' Walsh asked.

'Not since last autumn, but they'll be back in a few weeks, you wait and see. As soon as I've cut the corn. If the weather's fine, they'll be around, at all times of the day and night, too. It's not so bad once it's ploughed and sown and we've had a bit of rain – they don't like getting a bit of mud on their boots, you see. But it's the same with all the farms round here. The people taking their dogs for walks, or bird-watching, that sort of thing, they don't do no harm. You don't mind them.'

'Mr Nestor thought something happened up there about the time he moved in, some ten years or so ago. But he can't remember quite what it was, or who told him.'

'Good Lord, you're going back a long way. There were some nutters messing about, cock-fighting, or dogs maybe. I don't know how long ago it was. Maybe that's what he's thinking of.' He scratched his chin. 'Could be ten years, maybe less. Time flies. You might be better talking to them out at Wandlebury, there's things go on there, year after year.'

'I understand you were staying with your mother on midsummer's eve.'

'That's right. I go and see her at least twice a week and stay over, just to see she's all right. She's eighty-eight, you know, and still manages on her own, but it's worrying, when they're that age.'

'You're handy with the bowls, Nestor said.'

'Did he now? Yes, I like my bowls. Work hard, play hard, early to bed and early to rise, that's a farmer's life, you know,' he said, cheerfully.

'I've already told your young lady the other day; there's no way we can keep an eye on all the people that wander round the countryside,' old Mr Manton said, tapping his walking stick emphatically on the ground.

'I was rather more interested in what you might know about groups or societies that might use remote places for their services,' Walsh explained.

'Oh aye! There was some of them up at the old priory the other night, was there? I'd shoot the bloody lot of them, or send them to Siberia, or some such place. It were different in my young day. We didn't get the people from the towns come out here then, but they've all got motor cars now. In them days there was only just the local folk around, and everyone knew what each was up to. We didn't have no Mother Earth or Satan groups then. The Vicar would soon have put a stop to any nonsense like that. There's things go on at the Wandlebury rings, you know, but I'll tell you what,' he leaned forward confidingly and chuckled, 'we used to have some grand cock fights up there, in them old ruins on Privet's land, though it weren't his then. Rare fights them were, but that was before the war, and before you was born, likely. I mind there was something like that a few years back, but it wasn't local people, leastways if it was, they didn't tell me.'

'Mr Privet said something about some nutters in the priory, about ten years ago.'

'Might be. Ten years? Maybe, I'd have thought it was longer than that, but Privet wouldn't know a cock fight if he saw one, not him, with his church-going ways and his bowls.'

'He seems very keen on his bowls.'

'Oh ah! He's more keen on his stomach. He eats most nights in the club house or the pub, since he lost his wife. He hates cooking, does young Privet.'

Walsh had an hour or two to spare before he went to interview the high priest of the Satanists. He had driven down to the Mill. An impulse, because it was unplanned, but understandable because it was in his thoughts. There would be upwards of twenty uniformed or plain-clothed police officers about the city tonight, armed with photographs of Joanna Silvers and Martin Trent, and they would be visiting every pub, coffee house, restaurant or fast-food take-away; anywhere, in fact, where either of those two might possibly have called in during that fateful midsummer eve. He looked at his watch; it was nearly eight thirty, they should be hard at work by now. He leaned on the warm stone of the parapet and looked down at the river. The noise of the waterfall deadened much of the laughter and chatter of those that thronged the bridge. He turned his head. Yes, there were three of his men at the other end of the bridge. He could see heads move to look at the photographs and then shake, reluctantly. Well, it was not going to be easy to trace the last few hours in the life of Martin Trent. His eyes went back to the river: a man on a punt had lost hold of his long, unwieldy pole and was standing helpless and forlorn, as his craft swung round in the current, to drift downstream. He grinned at the sight, and headed back to his car, to go to pick up Brenda Phipps.

It was an impressive detached house. There was a wide, well-tended lawn, bordered by luxuriant shrubs and flower beds. The front door was opened by a lean, grey-haired man aged about fifty, who frowned down at them.

'You must be Chief Inspector Walsh,' he said.

'I am, and this is Detective Constable Phipps. You are Walter Dubonis, I presume,' Walsh replied.

Dubonis nodded. 'You'd better come in then,' he said, reluctantly, and ushered them into a pleasantly furnished sitting-room. A slender, dark-haired woman, wearing a long Indian cotton dress, rose to greet them. Her seemingly black eyes glared aggressively at them out of a pale, lean face with high, prominent cheek-bones.

'This is my wife, Hera. Hera, this is Detective Constable Phipps and Chief Inspector Walsh. Won't you both sit down?' Walter Dubonis said, with an icy politeness.

'Thank you,' replied Walsh. 'Mr Dubonis, we've spent

a long time talking to Mrs Haverston about the events which took place in the ruins of the old priory church at Barnhamwell on Midsummer's eve. We now know a certain amount of what went on, but we need to know more. For a start I need to complete the list of the members of your sect who attended. Mrs Haverston was unable to give us all the surnames and addresses,' Walsh stated, in a brisk businesslike voice. 'There's a man called Mike,' he continued.

Dubonis got up and walked over to a bureau by the far wall and took a book out of the middle drawer. 'Mike Thompson. 25, Arabian Meadows, Sawsthorpe. Anyone else?' he asked.

'Yes, and there's a Clive.'

It took several minutes to complete the list.

'Now, who was the little girl?' Walsh demanded.

Dubonis's face went pale and his wife suddenly started to bite a knuckle of her left hand.

'Little girl, Inspector? All our members are adults,' he replied.

'So they may be, but you took a child to your service. Mrs Haverston didn't know her name. What is it?'

'I told her not to say anything about that, she'd no right to tell you,' Dubonis said angrily.

'Don't be silly, Mr Dubonis. You left tracks all over the place. All of you. We knew anyway. What's her name?'

'Mrs Houndell's daughter, Gillian,' snapped Mrs Dubonis, 'but she took only a symbolic role in our service, I can assure you, Inspector. We are moderates, not extremists. There are many different degrees of belief, you know. We believe that his purpose for us has been mellowed by the development of our civilization and his wrath is now primarily aimed at those who deride or scorn him. It was only necessary to offer the girl to him; if he had wanted her, he would have put himself into the minds of his worshippers and taken her for himself, through them. It would be an insult to him to presume his actions, so it is our duty to offer whatever he might want, willingly.'

Walsh raised his eyebrows, trying to contain his surprise.

'No man commits evil of himself, you know, Inspector,' Mrs Dubonis continued. 'A visitation will be made for a specific purpose and he may take command of a body while he acts out his will. Then he will leave all as before until he chooses to use that body again. We cannot always understand his purpose, but we must be ready for him, when he needs us. And we must respect and nurture all life forms to ensure readiness for him to enter therein at his choosing.' Her voice rose shrilly. 'We are his people, chosen to serve him on this Earth, to willingly allow ourselves to be used for his wonderful purpose.'

'Hera, Hera! That's quite enough. I'm quite sure the Inspector isn't interested in such details.' Dubonis's face had turned quite red. 'All that Hera says is true though, Inspector. We do not need to denigrate those others of the spirit world, our services do not require the overturned Christian cross, for instance. We are not required to fight his battles for him. What good would we poor, weak mortals be to him who is all powerful?'

'If you are saying the child has come to no harm, then I hope you are right.' Walsh's voice held an underlying note of menace, and his eyes glinted steely hard. The attitude of the Dubonises seemed subtly to change from that moment, as though the menace in his voice and eyes had achieved, for Walsh, a respect that his presence and personality had failed to do.

'I want you both to think very carefully, and answer my questions truthfully. Have you ever used that ruined church before or do you know of any that have?' Walsh asked.

'No, that's the first time,' Dubonis said emphatically, 'and I don't know of anyone else using it, but then I wouldn't.' He looked at his wife, who shook her head.

'It was all right when we first went to look at the place in the daytime, but, well, there was an awfully strong confliction of forces that night, particularly later on. I've never felt anything like it before, yet our service was all right. I can only think we roused activity in some resident, hostile spirits, latent to that particular place. But why do you ask?' she said.

'I wanted to know if it was you that had cleared that area in the east end of the ruins.'

Dubonis shook his head. 'No, it was like that when we got there, but we'd have used it as it was, anyway,' he replied, with a puzzled expression on his face.

'Did anyone leave the service, even for a short period?'

'Good heavens, I don't think so. Certainly I don't recall the circle being broken during the initial rites, or the laudatory ones.' He looked at Hera for confirmation.

'No, Inspector, I'm sure no one left, not even for a short time.'

'Good. Now then, the order of people leaving, and the direction they went.'

It took some time and discussion between husband and wife before they had agreement. Walsh and Brenda waited patiently, occasionally making notes.

'What time did you leave the place?'

'I'm not sure exactly. I think it was just before two by the car clock, but we were definitely the last to leave. Us two, and Mrs Houndell and young Gillian. I had to carry her, she'd been fast asleep most of the time. We'd brought them with us, in our car, you see.' Now his attitude had changed from being coldly aggressive to being humble and helpful.

'We went back the way we came in. That would be along here.' He leaned forward to indicate his route on the large scale map that Walsh had laid on the floor.

'You say that Mrs Haverston and this Michael Graves left shortly before you, but by the same route, and that you parked your car next to theirs. Had they driven off by the time you got there?' Walsh asked.

'They were just leaving, in fact, we followed them most of the way back. They were driving rather slowly in front and Mike Thompson came up behind us. I know it was him because he waved as he cut outside us to go round the traffic island outside the Hospital. We went straight on, you see,' Dubonis told them.

'So you know of none of your party who might have returned for any reason? Perhaps someone left something behind, and went back for it?'

'No, but we had a good look round before we left. I couldn't swear to it, but there was certainly nothing obvious. No, as I say, there were our three cars all together driving home. I didn't see any of the other cars, but I wouldn't expect to, they would have gone a different way. I wouldn't have thought anyone would have gone back, though, not on their own. The place would have been very highly charged with the presence, you know, until it settled down. No, I doubt it very much.'

'The atmosphere you left must have been very evil, because the young man, Trent, was murdered shortly after you say you left,' Walsh said, grimly.

'Well, we had nothing to do with it, Inspector. I can assure you of that. As a matter of interest, how did he die? It doesn't say in the papers,' Dubonis asked.

'The boy was lying on his back. His throat had been cut

and a sharp piece of flint was in his right hand,' Walsh stated, bluntly.

Both of the Dubonises looked up in alarm.

'Oh my goodness!' Hera whispered hoarsely, looking at her husband in dismay. 'The demons of darkness. They must have been abroad at that hour, while his presence was still there, Walter. The sanctity of our service must have been defiled. He will be angry with us.'

'Be quiet, Hera. Do not say such things,' Walter Dubonis said in alarm. 'He will know it was none of us, and he will wreak his own vengeance on the perpetrators of this outrage and desecration.'

'Yes, Walter, but do consider. We chose the site, and we are responsible, both of us. The blame will fall on us, but all our members could be in terrible danger too, and so will anyone else that goes to that place,' Hera cried out, near to hysteria and quite distraught.

'No, Hera. Not now, for heaven's sake. There's nothing for us to concern ourselves about.' But his expression belied his words.

Walsh interrupted their argument. 'I would like to take away the shoes you each were wearing that night, if you please,' he said, coldly.

'What's that? Shoes? You want our shoes. No problem. Hera, you know which ones you were wearing, I don't. Would you go upstairs and get them? I was wearing those trainers I use in the garden. They're in the utility room. I'm sorry, Inspector, Hera does get a bit emotional at times. We'll do anything we can to help you bring this murderer to justice, I assure you,' he said earnestly.

Hera came back with the shoes in a plastic carrier bag. 'Here you are, Inspector,' she said, handing it to him.

'Thank you both. I may well need to talk to you again, but I'll ring you before I come if I do,' he said, as he and Brenda left.

'We meet some strange people in this job, Brenda. Quite how you describe this lot, I don't know,' he muttered as he drove down the road.

'You never said a truer word, Chief,' Brenda remarked. 'They certainly got themselves worked up about the possibility of Satan taking his vengeance on them, didn't they?'

10

'Joanna didn't want to come with us this year, Inspector,' Mr Silvers said, his drawn face pale beneath his suntan.

'It would have been better if she had,' his wife added, bitterly. 'You should have made her, Jim. You know I didn't like us leaving her on her own.'

'What's the chances of finding her – alive, I mean? Tell us the truth now,' Mr Silvers asked despondently.

Walsh looked down at his hands. 'There's still a possibility, of course, but the longer time goes on it seems less and less likely, I'm afraid. It might be that she went off to stay with this Jesus College undergrad named Wayne, who she was friendly with, but we haven't been able to trace him yet.'

'Him! I told Jo not to waste her time with him when she first came home talking about how she'd be going to a May Ball, but they don't listen, do they?' Mrs Silvers said. 'She was better off with young Martin, I told her so, even if he was a bit dull. He'd got a good job and was steady, but she would have it her own way, she had to learn the hard way. No! I don't think you'll find she's gone off with that Wayne, Inspector, she'd have taken some clothes and things with her, and I've looked in her wardrobe and drawers, pretty well all her stuff's still there. Besides, she wouldn't have gone without leaving us a note. She'd have known we'd worry.'

'You don't think she might have gone to spend a few days with any of her other friends or one of her relations, perhaps?' Walsh asked, hopefully.

'No! I don't think so. Her friends were all local girls, and I've already rung round our relatives. Besides, it's all in the papers, about her being missing, isn't it? She'd have been in contact somehow or other, if she could,' Mrs Silvers said, positively.

'So when this Wayne chap dropped her she tried to get back with Martin, did she? Weren't there any other boyfriends she might have taken up with?' Walsh inquired.

'Oh yes, there were plenty keen on her, there always has been, ever since she was old enough to be interested, but she'd got herself quite moody over Martin. I think she felt he'd come running back whenever she snapped her fingers, but he didn't. That upset her, hurt her pride probably,' the mother said, quietly.

'Can you tell me the names of any of the boys who might have made a play for her?'

'There was that Bill Smart from round Cooper Lane, he came round one evening and asked her out,' Mr Silvers replied.

'And Jackie Smith and Bob Watson, to my knowledge,' Mrs Silvers added. 'And that's not counting all the chaps where she worked.'

Walsh wrote names in his notebook; then said, 'It isn't likely they'll know any more than we do, but I'll get them checked out.'

'So Dubonis was one of the men wearing the same size trainers as Trent,' said Finch, his lanky body lounging in one of the easy chairs in Walsh's office. There was a pile of reports and statements on the coffee table beside him.

'That's right, his story seems to check out with what the people in the other cars say. It's a pity, I had him as a prime suspect,' Walsh replied.

'I think he still is, Chief,' Brenda remarked.

Walsh's eyebrows rose a fraction.

'Well, Dubonis was the last to leave, and he had a good look round, so he says, to make sure nothing had been left behind. Now, if he had seen Trent and Joanna hiding behind those bushes he could have crept up behind them, knocked them unconscious and tied them up. Then he could have carried on as he said, getting witnesses to him leaving, but he might only have driven to this point here,' she indicated a place on the map with a neatly manicured finger, 'then he could have got out, leaving his wife to drive the Houndell woman and her daughter home. The people in the other two cars don't actually say they saw Dubonis driving it, it was too dark for that. They assume he was there because it was his car.'

'Then Dubonis went back and killed Trent in that way because he had broken the sanctity of their ritual by spying on them,' Walsh added, thoughtfully.

'Yes, Chief, Mrs Dubonis would have come back, after dropping the Houndells off, to pick him and the girl up,' Brenda suggested. 'Mind you, that means Mrs Houndell was lying, but it's my opinion that she or any of them would, if Dubonis told them to.'

'It fits in with what we know, but why wasn't the girl killed, then and there, as well? Why take her away?' Finch asked.

'I don't know, but possibly killing a woman at that time might not fit in with their weird beliefs,' Brenda suggested, shrugging her shoulders.

'That might explain the expression on Dubonis's face

when I told them how Trent had been killed,' Walsh interposed. 'It didn't appear to be one of shock, not like his wife's reaction. That might have been because he hadn't told his wife exactly what had happened.' Walsh's eyes stared blindly at the wall while he recalled the scene in his memory. 'It could have happened like that. Anyway, unless Dubonis was remarkably careful, Forensic will find traces of Joanna in his car, then we'll have him. Until they've finished, we won't know.'

'There's another possibility we should take into account too, boss,' Finch remarked, quietly. 'Those people in the other two cars that left in this direction.' He pointed to the map spread on the coffee table. 'Going that way they might easily have seen the tracks Trent made coming in through the cornfield. They may have got suspicious, gone back, and found that Trent and the girl had been watching them.'

'That won't account for the set of trainer tracks from the other direction, Reg,' Brenda interrupted.

'Yes it will, if one of them was shrewd enough to realize they were leaving tracks as they moved about, and none of them are daft, are they? One of them could have put Trent's shoes on and taken the girl out in the opposite direction, then come back in a different way. Maybe he walked in backwards, just to confuse us,' Finch replied.

Walsh shook his head. 'I looked for that, toe prints deeper than heels and the irregular step constant looking over the shoulder would cause. No! I'm sure that wasn't the case.'

'But that would have meant that one of those two cars had to drive round to pick them up,' Brenda added, curling a strand of her hair with her fingers.

'Yes, and it could have been either car. Neither of the occupants actually confirms the movements of the others,' Finch continued.

Walsh leaned forward on the desk and studied his finger-nails. Both suggestions fitted the facts, but they were pure speculation, at the moment. It was difficult to put himself into the mind of someone who attended Satanic services. The normal criminal motives, greed, envy, passion and hate, these he could understand. In this case it was not so easy. There were sixteen or so persons involved, each and every one a bastion of city society. Dubonis was a director of a flourishing building company, well-educated, wealthy, and apparently respectable. His wife had been a State Registered nurse at one time, while Mrs Haverston was a schoolteacher, as also was Mrs Houndell. Thompson was an architect, and there were an accountant and a solicitor, as well as a garage mechanic and a plumber. Maybe later on he would be able to come to grips with their thoughts and emotions. It was easier, for the moment, just to toss ideas about.

'We mustn't forget there's the possibility that young Jeremy Fry and Wendy Jacklin were the other two,' he added. 'We know that Trent provoked Fry down at the Mill. What if they met up later, and somehow Wendy Jacklin was forced to go off with Trent? That would have made Fry pretty mad, and he's got that old motor bike at the College; he could have followed them, killed Trent with the spade in a fight, and brought Wendy Jacklin back with him. His shoe size is nine and a half, the same as Trent's, even though we didn't find he had the same make. Fry might have been wearing another pair that night and disposed of them.'

'The porter on duty that night was Jacklin's father and he remembers talking to Fry when he got back to the college at some time after eleven, Chief. Surely he would have said if Fry had gone out again, particularly with his motor bike,' Brenda commented.

'He didn't need to go out of the front gates. There's

another exit on to Downing Street that he could have used, if he'd got a key,' Walsh replied.

'That would mean Joanna Silvers has got nothing to do with Trent's murder. How do you account for her disappearance then? It's hardly likely to be just coincidence. Isn't it more likely that Rochester carried on down the Fulborn Road that night, after Mandy Street had got away from him? That would have taken him out towards Barnhamwell village. He could easily have gone out to that wood to look for the treasure, and met up again with Trent and Joanna purely by accident. He said he fancied Jo more than Mandy. Maybe he lost his temper again and got into a fight with Martin. We don't know for sure what time he got back to his digs,' said Brenda.

'He'd have been crazy to go treasure hunting at night, with no torch or tools, Brenda. He couldn't possibly have known that Joanna would be out there. So what would he have done with her, if you're right, after having killed Trent? Raped her, then led her away to kill her in cold blood somewhere else, then hide her body? Where?' Walsh asked.

'I don't know, Chief. One of the old chalk pits, the river maybe. We haven't finished searching them all yet.'

'That's right, we haven't, but we don't know where Tomkins was either. He didn't go to his local, that's for sure. He's hiding something. He could have gone after the treasure on his own; it's the kind of thing a fellow like him would do, too, like following up a sales lead, I mean. You'd better get him sorted out, Reg,' Walsh advised.

Finch nodded. 'And we'd better find who these Druid people are, boss, the ones who use the Wandlebury ring. They might have objected violently to the Satanists using a place too close to their own, and caught young Trent by mistake. That might explain why Joanna wasn't killed there, the Earth Mother might have objected to that.'

Walsh shrugged his shoulders. 'Can we ignore the possibility at this stage?'

'What about someone we haven't considered at all yet, Chief?' Brenda asked, her brown eyes looking shrewdly at Walsh.

'You mean someone not directly connected with the Satanists or Trent? Someone who just happened to be about at that remote spot at that early hour of the morning? You'd have to assume some entirely random motive, Brenda.'

'What about seeing naked revellers having an orgy? That might have flipped an unstable mind into sex and violence, though it doesn't explain the disappearance of Joanna. She'd have been assaulted and raped, I suppose, in which case one would have expected to find her body at the site as well,' Brenda suggested.

'Not if the person was an unstable male. He could have taken her away with him, keeping her a prisoner for a while. Didn't something like that happen in Cannock, a few years back?'

'Yes, Reg, and he turned out to be a multiple killer over a long period of time. I hate to think that we might have one like that, down here,' Walsh replied, anxiously.

'Maybe there's something in what Mrs Dubonis was saying about evil spirits being out and about,' Brenda suggested.

'They say there's a devil in all of us, waiting to get out. "Lead us not into temptation", the Lord's Prayer says. Maybe the temptation just happened to turn up in that place, at that time,' Finch remarked.

'We'll keep the evil spirits out of this, if you don't mind!' Walsh instructed. 'Reg, you go out to Wandlebury, and talk to the owners of the place. That might give us a new lead, and you've got Tomkins to sort out. Brenda, we don't know enough about Trent's and Joanna's friends yet. You work on those. There might be enough jealousy or rivalry amongst them to account for a murder. There're also the friends and relations of these Satanists to check out. One of those might have taken a dim view of what was going on, and tried to do something about it. In the meantime I'll have a word with Packstone. It's about time his team came up with their reports on the cars and clothing.' He reached out to feel the coffee pot, which was cold.

'It's all right, Chief, I'll get some more,' Brenda offered.

'It's a pretty unpleasant thought, you know, that Trent's killer may have got that girl hidden away somewhere. Not difficult to think of what he might be doing to her, either,' Finch remarked, when Brenda had left. Professionals though they might be, it was still easier to talk about some things when she wasn't there.

'I know, Reg, I don't like it either. Whatever way you look at it, this killer is quite cold-blooded. It's true, as Packstone said, that in a fight for the possession of a weapon such as a spade, the kind of swinging blow that cut Trent's throat might well have been unintentional, but there's no sign of rashness or panic in the killer's subsequent behaviour. Psychologically, that's worrying. He could kill again, neither should we assume this is his first time, either. I've got Records searching for any similarity in any of the unsolved murders during the past twenty years. When they've done that they can feed all the names involved into the "missing persons" computer. The truth of the matter is, though, we don't know enough about him yet.'

'Or her! A woman could wear size nine and a half trainers, but I don't see what else we can do at the moment, boss.'

'That's right, we must follow up what we've got, but we may find Joanna Silvers alive, and then it'll be easy. If we don't, we'll just have to plug on, regardless.'

Brenda Phipps came back into the office with a fresh pot of coffee. She put it on the desk.

'Thanks, Brenda, you're an angel,' Walsh said, smiling at the slim Detective Constable.

'With all this devil stuff about, the odd angel won't come amiss, boss,' Finch smiled.

'Less of the odd,' Brenda scowled.

The telephone rang. Walsh picked up the receiver. The other two gathered from his words that the doctors had found no signs of sexual abuse in their examination of Mrs Houndell's daughter.

'Thank goodness for that, that's one problem the less,' Walsh said, relieved. 'Reg, pass me those aerial photographs again.'

'There's a couple of these I'd like my own copies of, boss. See here on this one,' Finch pointed to an aerial print of the ruin in the wood, and the field to the south. 'The sun's low enough to throw crop shadows. The wheat grows better where the soil was once disturbed, less well where there're foundations beneath the surface. Barely detectable on the ground, but enough to throw a shadow when the sun's at the right angle,' Finch continued, enthusiastically. 'The dark marks here, along this side, could be the post holes of the wooden stockade that would have surrounded the priory originally, and these other lines are the foundations of walls. It's a pity the wood covers most of the site, we could've got a fair ground plan.'

'There're other marks on some of these photos too, Reg. What do they signify?' Brenda asked.

'This ring, here, might be a ploughed out burial mound, but these smaller marks are probably more post holes. It could be that the site was inhabited before the priory was built, but it would need a proper excavation before one could hope to identify the different occupation dates.'

Walsh interrupted. 'Very interesting, Reg, but I just want to see if we've missed any old chalk pits on our search plan. Keep the prints in order, don't get them mixed up.'

11

It was a tall, elderly, silver-haired lady who opened the front door of the big house to Reginald Finch.

'You'd better come in then, Sergeant. We can't stand here talking on the doorstep, can we?' she exclaimed, when Finch had told her why he had come.

'The estate was so much bigger, in my grandfather's day,' she said, pointing up at her ancestor's dark portrait over the fireplace in the spacious, chintzy sitting-room, and shook her head, regretfully. 'But so much of it had to be sold off when he died, for the taxes, you know. So you want to talk to me about the stone circle, do you? Now, is it a school party you want to bring, or are you doing a study of them at college?'

'Well, neither, actually. Like I said, I'm a policeman, and I'm interested in the Druids and their summer solstice ceremonies,' Finch replied, fondling the ears of one of the golden retrievers, which had come to rest its head on his knee and gaze up at him with soulful eyes.

'My grandfather had no time for the Druids. He was a general, you know, and used to say it was all poppycock and balderdash. Well, that's how they used to speak in those days, wasn't it? Now, Father had completely different views, much more liberal. I suppose it was because he was at Oxford when free-thinking became fashionable. He used to tell us girls what he said to a gentleman who actually came to ask permission to hold a celebration inside the ring. "I know there are more kinds of worship in this world than my own," he said, "but if you'll give me your word as a gentleman that there's nothing in your way that would give offence to me or to my wife, then you can hold your service." That was before we girls were born, but I believe a service has been held there every year since, except during the wars, possibly. I wasn't here then, of course.'

'Do you mean that you know who these people are? That they come each year?' Finch asked, in surprise.

'Oh yes, of course. Well, that is to say, the Leader comes each year, to ask permission, and he always gets the same answer, just as my father gave it. I suppose it's become our own little tradition, and I must say, on the few occasions I've watched them, they do keep to their word. It's a little like an ornate Harvest Festival service in long white gowns, really – without the fruit and vegetables, of course, but quite inoffensive,' she added.

'I'd very much like to talk to the Leader, myself, if I may. Do you know his name?'

' I don't, but my secretary, Miss Willis, is sure to. She only comes in on Tuesdays and Thursdays, so you'll have to come back tomorrow, won't you? Would you like another cup of tea?'

'Perhaps I might telephone her, instead, if you'd be good enough to let me have her number?'

'Of course. Was that one or two lumps of sugar?'

'You never went near that local of yours that night, so you've told me one lie already, Mr Tomkins. How can I be expected to believe anything you've said?' Finch asked, reasonably.

'It's easy to get things mixed up, and I'm sorry. Now

I've told you the truth. I came back here to the office that night, I had a lot of work to do on some softwear. Crikey, anyone can make a mistake, can't they?' the other replied truculently, his eyes glinting with anger.

'Well,' Finch said, 'I already knew that, as a matter of fact! Our patrols at night are pretty efficient, they take note of cars parked outside shops round here. Yours was outside at ten o'clock, but it wasn't there when they came round again at eleven. So you must have gone out again.'

'I went out for a coffee, yes, that's what I did.'

'Your coffee break lasted until nearly three o'clock in the morning then, did it? Because your car wasn't seen again that night, and there was no light on in the office at the back either. How do you account for that?'

'Easy! I parked it round the corner, in Riverside Road. Force of habit, I suppose, that's usually where I park during the day. As for the light, well, they wouldn't have seen it, because it wasn't on. The tube's on the blink and the flickering gives me a headache, so I worked just using the angle-poise on the desk.'

Finch got up, reached over to the wall, and switched the light on. After a few moments the tube lit up. It flickered and the starter buzzed noisily.

'Satisfied?' Tomkins scowled.

'Not really,' Finch admitted. 'You don't fill me with a lot of confidence. However, you might as well tell me who this urgent softwear was for.'

'Triton Roofing, they wanted the whole format of their sales analysis changed.'

'When did you give it to them?'

'Yesterday.'

Finch said 'Thanks,' got up, and walked out.

*

The fleeting expression of annoyance on Richard Packstone's face as Walsh opened the door signalled a warning.

'Five minutes, Richard? That's all. I just want to know how things are going,' Walsh said, apologetically.

Packstone sighed reluctantly, but lowered himself into his chair and leaned forward, with his elbows on the desk.

'It's pretty hectic in here,' he replied. 'I'm trying to get my priorities right, and at the same time keep everything else moving forward. So you'll have to be patient. I've got four people out with your teams searching the ditches, barns and old marl and lime pits; that's made me shorthanded, and there's the bits and pieces they're finding that need to be checked out. We've surface-examined five cars and a motor bike for prints for you, but we haven't even started the lab work on the minutiae from the interior scrutinies. We've not finished with the material from the priory site yet, you see, and it wouldn't be sensible to neglect identifying what might be important primary and positive data, would it? Brian, over there, is working on the hair samples you got from the Silvers girl's bedroom, though. It rather looks as if those strands we found on that bush near the ruins are hers, but he'll confirm that, in an hour or so.'

'They should finish searching the pits and ditches today, Richard. So you'll be back at full strength tomorrow.'

'Yes, but there're two burglaries and a fire at a primary school in Coton to do as well, but we'll manage. How are you getting on with your Satanists?'

'Steady progress,' Walsh answered, thoughtfully. 'The prime suspects are providing each other's alibis, unfortunately, and I'm having a problem finding the father of the young Houndell girl. I'm sure he wouldn't have been very happy if he knew his daughter was being used in their ceremony. He's suposed to be working on the oil rigs off Scotland, but even the National Insurance computers don't know where he is. Anyway, we may have a load more suspects yet. Reg Finch is out after the Wandlebury Druids.'

The wide open window let in the evening sun as well as the distant hum of the city traffic. The Chief Constable sat solidly in his chair, his plump face redder than usual.

'So what's the position with this Trent case, now, Sidney?' he asked.

Walsh rubbed his chin while he sorted his thoughts into logical order. 'Well! The search for Joanna Silvers hasn't been successful, not so far. We've had sightings from all over the country, as you'd expect, but none of them have been substantiated. She's not been seen for certain since she left that girl-friend of hers in the coffee shop in Regent Street on midsummer's eve, and went off with Trent. That's the last we know. I think the chances of finding her alive are getting slim.' Walsh pulled out his handkerchief from his trouser pocket and blew his nose, noisily. 'As far as the rest of the inquiries are concerned, we're still working on them,' he said, lamely.

'What! With all those suspects, Sidney? Haven't you got a line on any of them? You can't have drawn a blank, surely?' the Chief Constable asked, a note of irritation creeping into his voice.

Walsh restrained a caustic comment and patiently expounded a brief review of the facts.

'You seem to be getting on all right then, Sidney,' the CC remarked, after a few moments' thought.

'I'm not unhappy, not under the circumstances. Packstone's up to his eyeballs, that's not helping, and the scale of the search is tying up a hell of a lot of manpower. We'll have gone over an area of twenty square miles, by the time we've finished, and pretty intensively at that. We marked all the pits and outbuildings from those helicopter photographs. We even had it scan the whole area with the infra-red, heat-detector cameras looking for the body, but it hasn't worked, so far. I can't think that Finch'll turn anything up with the Druids, either, but it's worth trying.'

'Why not? Rival religious factions would be a good motive,' the CC asked.

'Well, the Druids' ceremony is at sunrise on the longest day, whereas the Satanists' is at night. It's hardly likely they'd meet up. No, our best chance of nabbing Trent's murderer is to find the girl's body. Forensic are still working on the Satanists' clothing and cars, but they've found no traces of the missing girl or the metal detector and spade that Trent took with him, yet. Much the same with Fry, Rochester and Tomkins, so there's no progress there either, and the scent's getting colder all the time.' Walsh paused to pour himself another cup of coffee.

'What else are you doing then?' the CC demanded.

'The murderer may have nothing to do with this treasure or the Satanists, and may be someone that just likes lonely walks in the middle of the night. So I've had patrols out there, with light-intensifier glasses, each night since we found the body, in case he goes back,' Walsh replied.

'I didn't know that, Sidney. Good thinking, though.'

'It will be, if it works, and it hasn't yet. The site visits are varied throughout the night. I've had patrol cars specially routed through that area, so I've been able to cover it without creating a special team,' he admitted.

The CC sighed.

'I don't see you can do much more, Sidney. Do you

think this is the sort of case where that TV series, Crime Watch, might be able to help?'

'I wouldn't have thought national publicity would be of great value to us.'

'You're probably right, but keep an eye on this Dubonis fellow. I was staggered when you told me about him. I've met him several times at charity functions and he's well thought of. It just goes to show, you never can tell about people, can you? Also this young man, Rochester, he's got a vicious temper. That report from his old school headmaster shows that.'

Walsh looked dubious.

'Maybe. Anyway, I've got some more research going on. This killer might just have done it before. We're looking to see if we can tie anyone involved in this one to an unsolved murder in the past.'

It was the CC's turn to look dubious.

'You'll have to do "missing persons" as well, Sidney, in that case. This character is clever. You can't find the Silvers girl's body, can you? He may be experienced at hiding bodies as well.'

'Yes, we'll have to, but it's a hell of a long job. Some of these people have moved here from other places, and it means finding out where they've lived, and getting old files dug out of archives.'

'The central computer can help. It's got to be done. Anything else?' the CC asked.

'I don't think so. Professor Hughes has asked me to pop in and see him sometime, but it didn't sound very urgent.'

'That's enough on this Trent case. I'll leave it to you to inform me when there's any progress. I want to have a word with you about these house break-ins. They're getting too frequent to be thought of as isolated incidents.

Have you thought of the possiblity that these are London-organized? It seems to me, though, that they've got inside knowledge, somehow. They all had the same kind of burglar alarms fitted, didn't they? And they're a London firm's installations. I know you've had their people checked out, but how if . . .'

The sun had nearly gone down by the time the meeting finished. Walsh felt in need of exercise, after sitting for so long, and a period of peaceful contemplation wouldn't go amiss. Walsh walked down to the city centre, and crossed the market square to Great Saint Mary's Church, then over the road to enter King's College through the main gates. He leaned on the river bridge, smoking a pipe and watching the ducks, boats and the people enjoying the pleasant summer's evening. Away over the other side of the great lawn, the last rays of the day's sun bathed golden the upper stonework of the lofty College Chapel.

12

Mr Stewart was tall and overweight, with thinning reddish hair and creases round his mouth that formed an interminable smile.

'The format of our services has no real historical basis, of course,' he said, with a chuckle, in answer to Finch's question. 'We can hardly use Caesar's Gallic wars account, can we? All that burning of victims in cages, that wouldn't go down well in our present society, would it? Mind you,' he continued more seriously, 'I don't believe half what he wrote, it smacks too much of denigrating propaganda for the folk back home in Rome to read, doesn't it? Tacitus was just as bad. Now other sources, like Pliny and

Posidonius, suggest the Druids were learned and peaceable. That's much nicer, so we can say they're the ones telling the truth, can't we?' His blue eyes watched Finch's face keenly, even while he laughed.

'How many years have you been involved in services at Wandlebury?' Finch asked.

'Well now, I took over from my father, twenty years ago it must be, but I was helping him for a good ten years before that. I was in the Army then.'

'And you've always asked permission from the Manor, each year?'

'Yes, it's almost part of the ceremony now. I love tradition, don't you? I always give the old lady a big bunch of flowers and invite her to come and join us.'

'You start your service to time with sunrise, I believe.'

'The main service, yes, we do.'

'The main service? What do you mean?' Finch asked.

'Well, as I said, the main service is at the time of sunrise, but a few of us come here to observe the state of the moon, half-way between dusk and dawn. You look surprised. Have you read Hawkin's study of the stones at Stonehenge and other places, showing how they were calendar observatories? If you haven't, you ought to. The precise relationship of the solstice to the lunar cycle is of vital importance during the rest of the year. You can see that, surely?'

'But why a ceremony? Can't you just observe, and be done with it?'

Stewart shook his head. 'No! The explanations to those without understanding are too complex and confusing. It's easier to tell them we're celebrating the shortest night and longest day as reflecting the relationship between evil and good, and do it then, just as the sunrise ceremony is merely to spot the longest day by observing the sun's position on the horizon, rather than a thanksgiving service.'

'So the lady up at the house doesn't know about the middle of the night bit, then?'

'Yes and no. It's part of our preparations, as far as she's concerned.'

'Does it end up with an orgy?' Finch asked.

Stewart grinned ruefully, and nodded. 'Usually! The younger ones do tend to get carried away with the idea of loving all our fellow creatures, but they do find themselves a bit of privacy first. No vulgar displays, I won't have that. Me, I'm getting a bit too old for that sort of thing, more's the pity.'

'Would many of them use the old Roman road to get here, do you think?'

'I don't myself, but some of them might.'

'I think you'd better give me the names. Can I have those attending the middle of the night service, first?'

Bill Smart's lean face was white and drawn, as though he had not been sleeping well.

'How long had you known Joanna Silvers?' Brenda Phipps asked sympathetically.

'You think she's dead, don't you?' Smart demanded, in a voice full of emotion.

'I don't know, honestly, but the longer she stays missing the more likely it is, I'm afraid.'

'But what could have happened to her? It's like a nightmare, not knowing.'

'You were very fond of her, were you?'

'I loved her, miss, and I don't care who knows it. Trust that stupid berk Martin to get her into trouble,' he growled, angrily, fighting back the tears that appeared in his eyes.

'So you knew him well too?' Brenda asked.

'Sure, he was in the year younger than me at school,

but I never liked him. He thought a lot of himself, but he wasn't so clever. Jo would still be alive if it weren't for him.'

'She might still be alive, and with him out of the way, you'd stand a good chance with her, wouldn't you?' Brenda suggested, watching his face keenly. She thought she saw a flicker of hope in his wet melancholy eyes, but it was difficult to be sure.

'I dunno, I dunno anything any more,' he replied, shaking his head.

'Just how well did you know her? I thought she and Trent had been going strong for quite a while, until recently, that is.'

'We'd been out lots of times, mostly with a crowd of others, but quite often just the two of us. That was a year or so ago, before she got going steady with Martin.'

'Where did you go, just the two of you?'

'All sorts of places. I took her to the theatre in Norwich once, she liked ballet, but pictures usually, in the evenings. A few times we spent a whole day in Ely, my dad's got a boat there. She'd sunbathe on the cabin top and mess about with the stove, cooking things, even though we'd taken sandwiches. We were getting on fine then, until bloody Martin decided to fancy her,' he told Brenda.

'It must be nice to have a boat of your own on the river, especially with the kind of weather we've been having.'

'We haven't used it much this year. Me dad's thinking of selling it anyway, he ain't been at all well lately.'

'You've got your own car, I suppose?' she asked.

'Yes, I passed my test first time. I've got an Escort now, with a 1600 engine. I did it up myself last year, well, with my dad's help I did,' he said, proudly.

'This boat of your dad's, what's it called, and where is it moored?'

She wrote his reply in her notebook. 'Now, where were

you on Midsummer's eve?' she asked, looking directly at his face.

'I went down the snooker club with me mates. I got home about half eleven. You can ask me dad, he was just going to bed when I got back,' he replied. After a few moments he started studying his finger-nails.

'What's your shoe size?'

'Nine and a half.'

'Your dad's at home, isn't he? That's all I want from you for now, Bill. Just ask your dad if I can have a quick word with him, will you?'

Later, she phoned through to Walsh. 'I'm popping down to Ely, Chief, I won't be long. I just want to check on a boat.'

The porter opened the door of the library, to let Walsh enter, and pointed to a corner desk.

'Thank you,' Walsh said, and walked over to where Professor Hughes sat, engrossed in reading a thick leather-bound volume.

'Hello,' Hughes said, his round chubby face smiling with genuine pleasure. 'It's good of you to come over.'

'How's the manuscript transcription going?' asked Walsh, politely.

'Come and see,' he replied, getting up and walking over to the small office where the work was being done. Jeremy Fry looked up as they entered and a fleeting expression of concern appeared on his face when he saw the Inspector.

'How's it going, then? Morning, Wendy,' Hughes said.

'We're getting on fine, Professor,' Jeremy replied, cautiously.

'Yes, I think you are. It's a long job and accuracy is essential.'

Walsh looked at the piles of dusty old deed boxes on the floor and the stiff, yellowed parchments on the desk and smiled at the two occupants. 'Discovered any more buried treasure?' he asked.

Wendy smiled up at him from the computer console and shook her head. 'I'm afraid we haven't. Sorry,' she told him.

'What's happened to John Rochester then, I didn't see him around?' Walsh inquired as he walked beside Hughes on the way up the stairs to the professor's rooms.

Hughes pushed open the door, and led the way into his sitting-room. 'We've dispensed with his services on this project, as a matter of fact,' he admitted, reluctantly.

'Oh dear! Can I hazard a guess that he couldn't leave young Wendy alone?'

Hughes raised his eyebrows in surprise, and nodded. 'Very astute of you. Yes, he nearly came to blows with young Jeremy, but Wendy's a sensible girl, and told us before it got out of hand. Now, I'll get some coffee ready, Inspector. You sit yourself down now, and make yourself at home.' He bustled through to a little kitchenette at the end of the room.

Walsh looked around. Nothing much seemed to have changed since his previous visits; a couple of the paintings on the long wall were different. He went to look at them. A pair of nautical paintings in oils: one was of a three-decked ship of the line under full sail. On the other, two frigates were engaged in battle, smoke billowing from their broadsides. The one flying the French tricolour was obviously having the worst of the exchange, its foremast had been shot through. The resultant tangle of canvas, rigging and spars hung precariously over the forepart of the main deck. There was also a suspicion of flame amidst the wreckage; either the ship was on fire or one of its carronades had just been discharged. The detail was incredibly clear for such a small painting; somehow the artist had even managed to convey a sense of confident activity in the tiny figures on the British frigate and an air of panic and confusion among the crew of the French ship. The artist's name he had never heard of.

'Good, that one, isn't it?' Hughes remarked as he came back into the room with a tray.

'It's very realistic.'

When they were both seated Hughes turned their conversation round to Barnhamwell Priory. 'The land on which the ruins are has belonged to King's College since the eighteenth century. The farmer is a tenant, as you probably know, but we found the manuscript, so they could hardly leave us out, could they? We're going to do a treasure hunt, together. I mustn't call it that, though. The fewer people that know, the better. No, we are going to do a proper archaeological excavation of the site, but what we are really going to be looking for is Brother Ignatius's "leaden box". Quite exciting, isn't it? A bit like part of an Enid Blyton story. The Famous Five in *The Secret of the Old Priory*! Sounds good, doesn't it? I've handled all the red tape myself, but you'd hardly expect any problem, would you? Not when King's and Downing of Cambridge make a request. We weren't sure which religious body might have jurisdiction over a ruined twelfth-century priory, so we told the Church of England and the Catholics that we were asking both of them for permission to excavate. I don't suppose they even knew the place existed. Anyway, there was no problem there. The department of the ministry responsible for ancient buildings merely asked for a copy of all the reports and findings when the excavation was completed, for their archives. So, it's all settled and set up, in just under three weeks, too – that must be a record in our bureaucratic society. There's just you and the farmer, to be informed.' Hughes broke off to drink the rest of his coffee. His eyes were bright with excitement and anticipation.

'You hardly need my permission, Professor, but under the circumstances I appreciate your informing me. One of my chaps is a keen amateur archaeologist – he'll be interested. So am I, for that matter. Why haven't you told the farmer yet?' Walsh asked politely.

'Because of the "treasured codex". We want to take no risk of that's being made common knowledge. The fewer local people that know about it, the better. I'm sure you can appreciate why we don't want the site invaded by hordes of people out with their spades and metal detectors. No, we decided to leave it to the very last minute. The surrounding fields will be harvested by the time we start, so access will be no problem. Ideal timing, in fact.' Hughes rubbed his hands together in gleeful satisfaction.

'I know that a codex is a manuscript, but what specifically makes this "treasured", do you think?'

'It's not just a manuscript, but a manuscript volume – book, in other words. In this case, probably more than one. We know very little about the activities of that particular priory, but we do know that one of its monks came over from Ireland quite early on, and that from that time they gained renown with the quality of their copying. All that remains of their work is a few fragments in the Bodleian Library. The illustrations on those fragments appear to suggest that it may be a direct copy of one of the beautiful Irish Bibles of the sixth and seventh centuries. The Vatican has the sole surviving example. Those Irish Bibles were themselves copies of the script of the Vulgate translation of the fourth century, but the illuminations, the decorations if you like, are pure Celtic masterpieces.'

'So because of that link with Ireland you think this codex might be one of those Irish Bibles? You may be right, but really, Professor, these aren't the dry, arid conditions of the Dead Sea area, not with our English climate. Surely nothing like that could have survived for over eight hundred years, not in our country. You could be heading for a big disappointment if you build up your hopes too much,' Walsh said, being ruthlessly practical. Hughes's face fell, his happy smile was replaced with a lopsided attempt at a rueful grin.

'I keep telling myself that, Inspector,' Hughes replied, slowly, 'but it doesn't take long for me to get back into an optimistic frame of mind again.' He spread his hands out in a helpless gesture. 'I'm supposed to be so coldly logical as well, that doesn't make it any better! It might be that the words "safe in the leaden box, tightly sealed" convey to my mind, in spite of my reasonings, that it could still be there. You see, Inspector, I've done a lot of self-analysis, but the possiblity of discovering such a Bible is of such importance that even a million to one chance must be followed up. Anyway, we shall see! You'll be very welcome to come to the site whenever you like and bring that man of yours who's interested. Yes, why not? You might be in at one of the major discoveries of the era, you never know.' His face had regained his look of happy enthusiasm.

'I shall have to cut out my night-time patrols,' Walsh said, half to himself. Hughes's eyebrows rose questioningly. 'One of the possiblities is that Trent's murderer happened to be at that particular place by sheer coincidence, when all the other Satanist people turned up,' Walsh explained. 'Anyway, I've been diverting traffic patrols out there every night to watch for such a person, but they've come up with nothing, so far. On the other hand, if he does exist, it might be very helpful if you could have a good night-watchman on the site.'

'I'm sure there will be, Inspector, but in the circumstances you could certainly have a word with him and tell him what to look out for, no problem there.'

'Yes, and I may issue him with one of our radios, then if anything does crop up, our men can get out there quickly. You might have a job getting someone to stay out there all night – the site of a murder can easily put funny ideas into the mind. I'm not talking just of the ghostly aspect either, there's a murderer at large somewhere. Anyway, if you get any problems in that respect, let me know. There're a few retired policemen about who might be pleased to help.'

'What was all that about a boat, Brenda?' Walsh asked, when she came into his office with Finch.

'It was just a hunch, Chief. I just had the feeling that this Bill Smart was overplaying the "I loved her and am so upset" act, and I think he smirked when he told me he'd been to the snooker club that night. He said he'd taken Joanna out on his dad's boat last year, and now his dad wants to sell it. So I asked if I could borrow the keys, and go and look at it.' She shrugged her slim shoulders.

'From the look of it you didn't find any sign of Joanna,' Walsh stated.

She shook her head this time.

'Never mind, good thinking! So you weren't happy that he went straight home from the snooker club?'

'Oh yes, I think he did, and his dad says he did, but he could have gone out again. His dad went straight to bed and went to sleep, apparently,' Brenda replied.

'You wouldn't be talking about a William Frederick

Smart of Wellesdene Gardens, would you?' Finch asked, as he handed over copies of his reports to the other two.

'Yes, I would, Reg. Why? What do you know about him?' she asked.

'Not as much as you, but I do know he went out again, because he was at the Wandlebury ring by about a quarter past two, next morning.'

'Chief!' Brenda exclaimed in excitement, 'if anyone had a real motive for getting rid of Trent, it was Smart. He'd been getting on pretty well with Joanna until Trent showed an interest, then she dropped him, but he was still keen, mighty keen. You know that, Mr Silvers told you how he'd been round trying to date her again.'

'All right, Brenda, I've got our interview report here. So Smart could have been in the area, but the timing is tight. Forget the missing girl for a moment. Could he have done it and been at Wandlebury for two fifteen? What do you think, Reg?' Walsh inquired calmly.

'Dubonis said they were driving home at a little after two, and it would have taken him a good ten or twelve minutes to get from the wood to his car, possibly a bit longer, since there were three of them and he was carrying the young girl. Trent couldn't have been killed before, say, a quarter to, or maybe even ten minutes to two o'clock. Then Smart would have had to go out as well, pushing Joanna along in front of him, by the same way as Dubonis did. We don't know where in the lane Smart's car would have been parked, do we? Never mind, there's about four miles of country lanes from there to Wandlebury – say ten or twelve minutes. It's tight, but it could be done, I think. We ought to get someone to do it and time them,' Finch suggested.

'Yes, yes, later, Reg. So the timing's a possibility. But Smart would have had to be going along the Roman road, or else he could never have spotted Trent, or his car. Agreed?'

He waited for the other two to nod before continuing: 'So the first question is, why didn't he follow Trent and the Silvers girl directly across the field? We know that Smart, or whoever it was, went in from the other side of the wood, and he and Joanna left that way. So why did Smart drive all the way round? That must have taken him at least a quarter of an hour, if not longer, don't you think?'

'Maybe there was another vehicle behind him, Chief? Another of the Druids, possibly,' Brenda commented.

'You've not spoken to any of these names on the list, other than Stewart, presumably, Reg?' Walsh inquired.

'Not yet,' Finch said, shaking his head.

'Let's take the position further, then. The Satanists go off and Trent and Joanna come out of hiding. Then Smart comes in and there's an argument and a fight, which Trent loses. Joanna wouldn't have been too happy at that, and I can't imagine her protesting quietly. Nevertheless, Smart picks up the spade and metal detector and takes them and Joanna back to his car. He ties her up and gags her, puts them all in the boot and calmly drives off to the first Druid service. Was he there at the sunrise one as well, Reg?'

'Yes, he was.'

'So the girl would have been in his car boot from just after two until seven or eight o'clock in the morning. He'd have to be a mighty cool customer, this Bill Smart. He couldn't have risked keeping her in the boot all that time, while still alive, surely. So he must have killed her first. Then I suppose he drove straight to Ely and took his dad's boat out, dropping her body and the other things in the river somewhere. Yet he was supposed to love her.'

'If Smart saw part of the orgy and then watched the girl

he loved willingly let Trent do to her all the things he desperately wanted to do to her himself, then that love might rapidly have become blind hate, Chief,' Brenda suggested.

'Maybe, but the signs were there that Trent had treasure hunting in his mind, not sex,' Finch argued. 'We'll leave reading these reports until later, I think. Brenda, get Packstone to check Smart's car. As a proposition, it's full of holes, but I've heard worse. Reg, get those people on the first Druids' meeting list seen. You'd better give him a hand, Brenda. If there's a single item of corroborative evidence, we'll pull Bill Smart in for questioning.'

13

Brenda Phipps had slouched herself down comfortably in one of Walsh's visitors' chairs, and had read through several new reports by the time Finch and the Inspector arrived. Both looked slightly dejected.

'No luck with young Smart then, Chief?' Brenda deduced, as she pushed herself upright.

'No, blast it. Can't get him to budge,' Walsh admitted as he sat down at his desk. 'As soon as we told him that one of his Druid friends told us that he'd driven behind him all the way along the Roman road, he came clean, as far as that was concerned. He said he didn't tell you he'd gone out again because he didn't want to admit being a Druid.'

'But he didn't admit seeing Trent's car though?'

'No, he said it was dark and it took all his attention missing the potholes.'

'But what was he doing going out there so early then, Chief?'

'The same as the other fellow, Brenda. Neither dared to risk going to bed that night in case they overslept, and they both got fed up mooching about at home, that's why they were so early,' Walsh informed her.

'But what explanation did Smart give for arriving so much later than the chap who was following him?'

'He says he pulled off the road into a copse just past where the Barnhamwell track comes in on the left, and had a smoke. That's his story and he's sticking to it. He'd never heard of Barnhamwell Priory and had never been there in his life,' Walsh said, ruefully.

'And we've got nothing to prove otherwise,' Finch chipped in, 'unless friend Packstone can find a link.'

'Did he get very emotional? Did you think he was overdoing it?' Brenda asked.

'He certainly got emotional, didn't he, boss?' Finch replied. 'Tears most of the time, but I wouldn't have said he was acting though. He's not tough enough for that, in my opinion.'

'Not like your friend Tomkins, then, Reg,' she smiled. 'I've just been reading your report on the last time you saw him. He really got under your skin, didn't he?'

Finch scowled. 'Too right. He's a habitual liar, that one. I wish there was something concrete to tie him in with the missing girl. I'd enjoy grilling him,' he said, maliciously.

'He's the sneaky type, Reg,' Walsh interposed. 'He might kill for money, I suppose, at a pinch, but he's much more likely to lift your wallet when you're not looking.'

'He was up to something shady that night, boss. I'm sure of that,' Finch replied, getting up to hand out the coffee cups which Walsh's secretary had just brought in and placed on the desk.

'To change the subject, Chief, I know I'm not working

on your burglary cases, but a couple of reports have got mixed up with the Trent papers, and I've read them. Is there a consistent pattern to make you think they're all by the same gang?' Brenda asked, as she put her empty cup back on the tray.

'It's the CC who thinks there's a gang of them, Brenda. It could just as easily be someone on his own. Yes, the same pattern. Each place has been fitted with the same type of modern computer-controlled alarm, with sensors in most of the rooms that would detect anyone moving about when it was switched on. The door at the side of the house, usually the kitchen one, is always the designated exit point, with the control box just inside,' Walsh explained. 'He gets in by removing the bottom door-panel. Uses a jigsaw, if it's wood; if it's glass, he levers the beading away and takes out the glass. Very neat.'

'How does he immobilize the alarm then?'

'He uses a disc cutter to make a hole in the control box, then we think he inserts a couple of probes connected to some electronic gadget, which enables him to bypass the set program and render the alarm inoperative. Even the manufacturer can't work out how. He takes lightweight valuables: money, jewellery, silver, that sort of thing. No prints, no traces. Why do you ask?'

'This report I've just read is of the questioning of a neighbour of the one that got done the night Trent was killed.' Brenda reached across the desk to give Walsh the document. 'The woman thought she saw a grey car go by when she put the milk bottles out. Tomkins has a grey car and is a computer expert. It could be him, couldn't it? That'd be a good alibi for Trent's murder, wouldn't it?'

'Middling fair,' Walsh replied, thoughtfully, and reached for the phone.

*

'That was an excellent meal, my dear,' Mr Jacklin said to his daughter, as he held a lighter to the bowl of his pipe.

'I can't recall when I've eaten a better, Mr Jacklin,' Jeremy Fry added. 'She could teach the cooks in College a few things too, I shouldn't wonder.'

'Probably, but I can't stay sitting here, unfortunately. I've got to get myself ready for work. I'm sorry I haven't time to do the washing up before I go, but you can leave it and I'll do it in the morning, if you want to go out,' Mr Jacklin offered.

'As if I'd do that, Dad. You know that you'll be dead tired, you always are, especially the first night of your night shift,' Wendy said, indignantly.

'Please yourself, love,' he said, pushing his arms into his jacket and walking towards the door. 'I'll say goodnight now. I'd better get off.'

After he'd gone, Jeremy insisted on helping. He'd do the washing, he said, since he might drop things if he had to dry them; besides, he added, Wendy knew where everything went, so she could put them away at the same time. It wasn't really a chore, doing things together, just her and him, Jeremy thought, but after a while he sensed that Wendy had become a little preoccupied. A slight furrow had appeared between her eyebrows. At first he thought it might be that she was a little concerned, now that she was alone in the house with him. That would have been a perfectly understandable explanation, but he began to think it might be more serious than that. He pulled the plug out of the sink and watched the dirty water drain away before wiping round with the cloth and rinsing the bowl.

'Wendy, you've got something on your mind and it's worrying you. What's the matter?' he asked, sympathetically.

She looked at him, a little surprised.

'Oh, it's nothing really.'

'Well, if it's nothing, you shouldn't have that groove between your eyes. Come on, what's the matter?' he demanded, coaxingly.

She took his arm and led him to the settee in the sitting-room and sat down. 'All right, I'll tell you. It's just that I keep thinking about poor Martin Trent. How if he hadn't overheard us talking, then he would never have gone out to that place and he would still be alive today. I've got this feeling in me that it was all my fault, and I can't seem to shake it off.' Her face looked very distressed, now that she'd spoken about it.

Jeremy thought for a moment before replying. 'Wendy, there was a whole sequence of events that took place that night. We were only one of those, and a minor one at that.'

'Oh, Jeremy, how can you say that? He would never have gone out to Barnhamwell if he hadn't heard me talking.'

'Yes, but if I hadn't used that X-ray machine we would never have known that there was anything else written on that manuscript. So if we use your logic, I'm more to blame than you are, for finding out about it in the first place. Or you could blame poor old Ignatius for writing it, or the chap that sold Martin the car that he drove out there.'

Wendy shook her head as she began to smile at Jeremy's simple reasoning. 'Silly. You're just trying to put my mind at rest, aren't you. Well, that's very kind of you, but in spite of what you've said, the fact still remains that he's dead because I opened my big mouth. I feel guilty about it, Jeremy. I know all the things you are going to say, but they won't make any difference, because nothing can alter the facts. It's been on my mind for days now.'

Jeremy took her soft warm hand into his, and pressed

it reassuringly. His instincts warned him that his natural reaction, to make light of the matter, wasn't appropriate in this case. So he tried another line. 'What you feel is quite understandable. I've had a few similar twinges myself,' he admitted. 'What we need to do is to get the whole thing properly into perspective. Although young Martin learned of Barnhamwell from us, his decision to go there was entirely his own, and it's very unlikely that we could have persuaded him to change his mind, even if we could have known what he was planning to do. So from that point of view he must take a lot of the blame himself. You must agree with that.'

Wendy nodded, partially convinced.

'So!' he continued, 'all we can do is say "sorry" in some way for the part that we played. He wasn't a bad chap, you say, so even if he was a bit upset that night, he wouldn't bear a grudge against us personally. What about us putting some flowers on his grave, and saying "sorry" that way?'

'You make it sound so straightforward, Jeremy. I know I'm just being silly, but doing something would help put my mind at rest, I think,' Wendy replied, uncertain nevertheless.

'That, and time could do the rest. It's not a thing that either of us will ever forget completely, but we must make sure that it doesn't upset our lives for the future,' he said confidently.

'I suppose you're right, but not flowers on his grave, Jeremy, that won't do. It's got to be flowers where he died, where his spirit left him. It stands to reason, that's the proper place. Would you take me out there tomorrow evening? I know it's very silly of me, but that's what I'd like to do.'

Jeremy looked anything but pleased at the idea, but he realized he'd talked himself into it. 'If that's what you want, Wendy, then of course that's what we'll do. I'll have to borrow a crash helmet for you, and check my motor bike over. It's a bit past its best and can get temperamental at times, but it'll get us there and back all right. We'll get some flowers tomorrow, then, but I wouldn't tell your father about it, he'd only worry, and if he's working nights all this week he doesn't need to know,' Jeremy suggested, his face even more serious than usual.

'We could leave just after he goes off to work, couldn't we? It won't be too dark by then and it won't take us long to get there, will it?' Wendy said. It might stop those horrid dreams she'd been having recently. It was worth a try, anyway.

There was just room for a fifth car to squeeze into the gap beside the garage, although the passenger found that her door was opening very close to the roses that were being trained to climb up the brickwork of the wall. She frowned as she unhooked thorns from her loosely knitted white cardigan, but the frown might have been the result of thoughts that had no connection with the beautiful white blooms, whose fragrance floated so seductively in the warm evening air.

She had been surprised by this unscheduled call to meet tonight, in fact she had been surprised that there was a call at all. In her mind she had become quite convinced that the group would break up after the events following last month's service. That would be a pity, even if it was a shame that so many other women had joined these past few years. When she had first gone along there had been only three other girls for all of the nine or ten men. That had been in the sixties, of course. She'd never forget the first service she went to. The men had let her drink far more whisky than an innocent sixteen-year-old could possibly handle, all the new girls got that treatment, but she had danced with such joyful abandon, and got so excited and proud of the desire her firm young body was obviously creating. She had given in completely to the frenzy of the dances, every pore of her skin had absorbed undreamed of sensations of pleasure, but that had been nothing, compared with what was yet to come. She'd screamed and screamed in the ecstasy of those tremendous climactic triumphs. No man had ever been able to achieve that effect on his own, since. Perhaps that had been the real cause of the failure of her two marriages.

Mrs Haverston followed Mike Graves into the sitting-room. They were the last to arrive and the settee and all the chairs were occupied. So she sat down on the floor, leaning back against the side of one of the armchairs, putting both her arms round her raised left knee, trying to appear unaware that she was exposing a view of her bare thighs to those sitting on the other side of the room. She felt a light flush come to her face and glanced up. Mike Graves was looking at her, so was John Buxton. She gave them a long steady look and a brief smile.

'My friends,' Dubonis said, raising his hands to quell the chatter. 'My friends. Let me explain why I have brought you here. As you all know, last month's service was defiled by the subsequent death of that young man. We had called his presence there and offered ourselves, as is our duty, but someone, unknown, raised an insult to him in that place. We have given much thought to what to do, both to cleanse the site and to ensure that we are absolved from any suspicion of sin, and we have decided that we must return on the night of the next full moon to abase ourselves in supplication and to reinitiate ourselves. It will be a short service of course, and the presence of a juvenile will not be required. White cloaks must be worn all the time, for we will need to have a clear sign before we may demonstrate our delight in his presence. Tomorrow night then, my dear friends, at midnight. Take very great care not to be seen approaching that place. We must not have our service interrupted, and you must all be there, it must be as it was before. You must not fail. Then we can raise this ugly spectre from our minds and once again, we can set about preparing ourselves for the great coming, at which time all truths will be made known. Now, there's coffee or drinks next door in the dining-room. Don't be late to bed tonight, you'll need to be fresh tomorrow.'

Mrs Haverston fumbled to find the right key to the front door of her flat. She pushed the door open and hurried through into the sitting-room, kicking off her shoes and unbuttoning her blouse as she went. She pulled the curtains closed and turned, smiling radiantly. Mike Graves and Alex Finder stood quite still, watching intently, as her clothes were thrown carelessly to the floor. Her eyes dilated as she glided seductively towards them, her tongue licking her lips and her arms held out.

'Suspect's come out of the shop by the back way and is getting into his car,' reported G1, from his position in the side street.

Walsh drummed his fingers on the desk and his eyes looked up from the radio link console to the faces of his two assistants.

'He's going home probably,' he muttered, and reached forward to press a switch. 'G3 and 4, start moving towards the junction now. He should be pulling out in front of one of you any moment now.'

'G4, he's heading towards the Huntingdon Road.'

'G2! Get moving. G4! Follow if he turns into town. G3!

Cut round to the Grantchester Road. G1! Cover the Chesterton Road,' Walsh instructed.

'He's not going straight home, from the look of it,' Brenda said quietly.

'We'll be damned lucky to catch him on the first night's surveillance,' Finch added.

'G2, I'm with him now, he's crossed the traffic lights and going up Castle Hill.'

Walsh picked up his hand radio and stood up. 'Keep with him, G2. G4! Stay well back.' He stuffed his pipe into his pocket. 'Come on, you two. It's time we were moving.'

They hurried down to the car park. Brenda got behind the steering wheel and drove, fast, westwards.

'G2, he's turning right, to Girton.'

'G2! Go straight on, then turn and follow. G4! Take over. G1! Head towards Histon,' Walsh ordered.

'G4, he's gone through the village. We're on the Histon Road now. Ah! He's turning left, Mandell Lane.'

Walsh's finger moved an inch to the right on the map folded on his knee.

'Follow then, G4. Mandell Lane leads back to the village from the west, but there're several turnings off,' Walsh warned.

'G4, he's taken the second right, just saw his rear lights.'

'That's Shudy Lane! It only leads to a farm, about half a mile away, but there're several big houses before then. He can't get out without you spotting him. Proceed on foot, G4. Home in to Mandell Lane, the rest of you.'

'G4, I can't see him. The road bears to the right after a couple of hundred yards. He must be up there, unless he's pulled in to one of those houses.'

'Wait till I get there then, G4.'

Cloud covered the moon and it was very dark, there

were no street lamps out in that country lane. The wind rustled the leaves in the tall trees, although at ground level the air was still.

Shudy Lane was bordered on either side by broad mown verges.

'You two go up the other side with Reg, we'll do this side. We'd better get a move on. I want to catch him at it.'

They moved quietly away; dark silent shadows, keeping close to hedges and fences. The houses stood in spacious grounds. Tall trees, mature shrubs and bushes gave seclusion and privacy, from each other, as well as from the road.

'He's in the fourth on the right, boss,' Finch's voice whispered over the radio.

They gathered near the entrance.

'There's no lights. The side door will be down there by those garages most likely. That's the way he'll have gone, but you four cover the other three sides,' Walsh directed.

The bottom panel of the side door had been neatly cut away. Walsh and Finch positioned themselves on either side of the door, with their backs to the house wall, far enough away not to be seen by someone coming out. Brenda's slim figure slid between a laurel bush and the garage wall, directly opposite, her torch held ready to illuminate the scene. Then all that was needed was patience, and that those waiting had in plenty.

Some twenty minutes elapsed before they heard the rustling and clink of a bag being pushed through the aperture, but no move was made until the figure had crawled, on hands and knees, after it. Brenda's torch came on and two pairs of strong hands ensured that no escape was possible.

14

'Well! I must say that's very good work, Sidney, and you caught him in the act, that'll make the Prosecutor's job a lot easier. No chance for Tomkins to wriggle out of that,' the Chief Constable said, with considerable satisfaction. 'What put you on to him, though? Last time we spoke about these burglaries it was all generalities, you'd nothing to go on.'

'It was young Brenda. She related Tomkins grey car to the grey car seen by the neighbour at the burglary on the night of Trent's murder. Packstone had gone over Tomkins's car, so I asked him to look for any connection with the break-ins. He found some hairs in Tomkins's car that were compatible with a single one they found caught in the rough edge where the bottom panel of the door had been cut out. So we had three tenuous links, car, computer know-how and the hair. Not good enough to get a conviction, but worth putting him under surveillance. We were lucky he set out to pull another job so soon,' Walsh replied, rubbing his eyes and stifling a yawn.

'Brenda Phipps, eh? I didn't think you were using her on that case.'

'I wasn't, she's plenty on her plate as it is. No, some reports got mixed in with the Trent file, that's how she knew that the neighbour had seen a grey car.'

'Good thinking though. You always said she was a bright one.'

'She is; and you'll find her recommended for a move up the ladder on the next review list.'

'I will, will I? We'll see.' the CC remarked, scratching

the side of his head thoughtfully. 'Has this Tomkins owned up to the previous break-ins?'

'Not yet,' Walsh replied, 'but he will, when he's had time to chat with his lawyer.'

'You think so?'

'Yes, pretty certain. That little electronic gadget he'd made, it ties him in with the other jobs too neatly. You know he cut a small hole in the metal cover of the control box and used two probes to make contacts in just the right places. The display on his gadget showed those numbers that had been energized when the alarm was set. All he had to do was tap those into the control box; that switched it off, and with it all the internal sensors that would have given him away had he tried to wander from room to room,' Walsh explained. 'But what I like best in his tool kit is his Black and Decker jigsaw, modified with a "cordless drill" motor. It's so quiet, you can hardly hear it at all if you're more than six feet away.'

'Clever sod, is he? But that lets him out of the Trent case, I suppose,' the CC admitted reluctantly.

'Yes, I'm afraid it does. Other than the Satanists, Smart's the only one we can prove to have been in striking distance of the old priory, but we can't pin him down, yet. He's got the best motive but he's not the right type, whereas Rochester is.'

'Perhaps you should try Rochester against some of the rape and sexual assaults we've had since he came up to the University. Maybe you'll strike as lucky with him as you did with Tomkins,' the CC suggested.

'Well, I'm having the data on all of them, and the college dons and the Wandlebury mob, re-checked from scratch. Maybe something'll come out of that. We still can't find Mrs Houndell's ex-husband, but we think he may have got work on the Dutch drilling rigs, so we've asked them to help. On a wider front, we're still working on "unsolved murders", "sex crimes" and "missing persons", but it's a long task, that. The computers can only cross-reference the names of those specifically concerned, there's just not enough detail in the data banks. It's got to be done the hard way. All the reports and submissions in all those files have got to be read through if we're going to find any connection or reference to the names on our "involved" list.'

'Being methodical and patient is the only way, sometimes. Have you still got your people going out to the priory during the night?' the CC asked.

Walsh nodded; this time he couldn't stop a yawn. He'd only managed to get a couple of hours' nap that morning, after he'd finished interrogating Tomkins. He should sleep well that night.

The moon was bright, but at times it was obscured by patches of cloud, so that at one moment it was possible to see quite well, then the light would disappear and darkness took hold of the land again. For the most part, the fields had been shorn of their crops, exposing to view the broken flints and the chilly white of chalky lumps, between dry rows of stubble.

The watcher was concealed behind a row of round straw bales that lay stacked in the corner of a field. From this point he could observe a wide area. To the south, the ground fell gently into a low valley, then rose to peak at the clump of trees silhouetted against the dark sky. Across the field in front of him a dark shadow was slowly passing as a cloud crossed the moon. He rested the night glasses on a bale and looked round, behind him. His Panda car was well concealed in a little copse, down there, to his left. It was a spot he had found several weeks ago, when this night patrol had been started. It had been handy to the narrow track that provided the access to these fields for farm vehicles, and wasn't very far from the 'B' road that wound itself round the low hills and joined up with the main road some miles to the east. It was as good a spot for watching as you could hope for in the open countryside, and there was a tolerably good chance that these random visits during each night had passed unobserved. The watcher didn't mind this duty. He was used to long uneventful periods on patrol and in a way this was fun, behaving a bit like the Boy Scout he had been when he was young. There was a freshness, too, in the gentle breeze of the night air that bore a subtle hint of the fragrances of the wild flowers of the hedgerow. It brought something else too, the faint droning throb of a car engine in the distance, rising and falling gently, but coming nearer. The watcher looked at the time. He'd been there for quite a while now, however; he would wait for this car to pass. There had been little enough activity to be observed over these last few weeks; an occasional courting couple or dog walker, nothing else. The engine note had changed in some subtle way. He turned his head slightly to try and focus on the sound better, perhaps there was more than just the one car. He settled down to wait, so motionless and silent that other, more tiny creatures of the night felt safe to continue their normal activities.

One of the cars was coming slowly up the track behind him, he could see the glow of dipped headlights. It turned into the entrance of a field and became silent, so that the watcher could concentrate on the other sounds. Only momentarily, because the sound of car doors being slammed came like rifle shots in the stillness. He fingered his radio and extended the aerial to its full length, ready for use. The hum of voices, talking low, in half-whispers, was carried on the air. They had passed the copse that hid the Panda car; now he could see them walking, half-crouching, close along by the hedgerow that would lead them to the small wood. Now was the time to report in.

'R5, to HQ. Reporting activity at the old Priory site. Observed, three people making their way there now. Other vehicles in the vicinity, heard but not observed,' the watcher whispered.

'Panda, R5, your message timed at twenty-three thirty-five hours. Stay and observe, repeat, remain in present position.' The watcher turned the volume down as low as he dared, wedged the instrument between the bales, and took up the night glasses again.

Inspector Walsh was ready to go upstairs to bed when his wife answered the telephone, but the news of nocturnal visitors to the Barnhamwell Priory site changed all that. A few rapid instructions were all that was necessary and then he was kissing her goodbye and hurrying out into the darkness. By the time that he had met up with Brenda Phipps and Reginald Finch, the owners of the vehicles now at the priory site had already been identified by the extra patrols he had diverted into the area. Dubonis and his group were out to hold another midnight service. Well, this time their movements would be closely monitored. He had given instructions to his men to keep out of sight and not to approach the ruin. They were only to apprehend anyone who might leave, until he could be there in person and take charge. He made good time, avoiding the Roman road and coming in on the northern side, following the route of the watcher. After a few words, Walsh left him at his post and made his way along the hedgerows out to the ruin, followed by his two assistants. Before entering the wood he inserted the ear-plug lead into the radio and disconnected the speaker, and checked that his torch was handy in his pocket. Then they found a place where they could see and hear all that was happening.

Wendy was so quiet during the evening that her father asked her if she was feeling all right. She assured him that nothing was the matter save a slight headache, and so Mr Jacklin continued describing to Jeremy the motor bikes he had owned in the past, until the time came for him to set off for the college to do his stint as the night porter at the main gate. Wendy then went upstairs to change her clothes for something more suitable for a girl on the back of a motor bike, so that it was already getting late by the time they eventually set off. Jeremy had checked over his old motor bike during the day, but since he was not particularly mechanically-minded, this took the form of oiling anything that moved and tightening any of the nuts that he happened to find a spanner to fit. Nevertheless, everything went well until they had turned on to the old Roman road. There the nipple came off the throttle cable at the twist grip, and they rolled to a standstill. Wendy laid the bunch of flowers she had been cradling in her arms down on the grass and listened to Jeremy's explanations.

'It's not your fault, of course, but isn't there anything you can do? I don't fancy being stuck here all night, or walking home, for that matter.'

Jeremy thought for a moment, trying to apply basic common sense to the problem. Eventually he made a decision and took his small bag of tools from the cavity under the seat. He loosened the bolts of the clamp that held the front brake lever to the handlebar on the right-hand side, pushed in the loose end of the throttle cable and retightened the bolts. By pulling on the black outer cover of the cable, he could operate the throttle to some degree.

'It's worth a try,' he said, really rather pleased with himself. He started the engine and rode it successfully along the track a little way.

'I think we'll be all right. Come on, get back on again.'

Wendy looked relieved, and picked up the bunch of flowers again. 'Better take it slowly,' she suggested. With all the ruts and the bumps in the road, Jeremy didn't need telling that. Wendy found time to appreciate the dark stillness of the night, occasionally bathed in the pale glow of the full moon. After a few bumpy, wobbling miles, Jeremy braked to a stop, his feet scraping on the dry hard surface for the last yard or two, and took off his helmet.

'That's it, over there, I think,' he said, pointing to the far clump of trees across the fields.

'Good, I shan't be sorry to be on our way back home.' She looked around. There was no sign of a living soul and no sounds other than those caused by the gentle breeze in the leaves of the hedgerows. The motor bike was put up on its stand where it was; there seemed no point in wheeling it off the road. Had he been on his own, Jeremy might have ridden across the fields right up to the wood, but with Wendy there, it wouldn't be wise. So, with Jeremy carrying a torch in one hand and with the other holding Wendy's arm, they made their way over the fields, their feet making swishing noises as their shoes brushed through the stubble. At the edge of the wood they looked for an easy passage and found a narrow gap through the entangled briers. Wendy stepped carefully through the undergrowth. Suddenly she heard the sound of voices. She stopped abruptly, and turned, opening her mouth to speak. A shadow rose from the darkness behind her. A hand was clasped over her mouth and a strong arm encircled her body, trapping her arms to her side.

The flowers fell to the ground as fear momentarily paralysed her limbs of movement. She started to struggle but a voice whispered softly in her ear, 'Quiet, we're police, don't make a sound.' A face came close to hers. In the gloom she made out the features of the Inspector she had met in Professor Hughes's rooms. She nodded as well as she could within the encircling arm. The grip loosened and on trembling legs she followed the Inspector as he beckoned her out of the wood.

Jeremy was already there, his face white and strained, rubbing his shoulder as he sat on the ground. Brenda picked up the fallen bunch of flowers and a white card that lay where it had fallen. In the moonlight at the edge of the wood, she could just read the words on it: 'We are so sorry, Martin. But it was not really our fault. Please rest in peace. God bless. Wendy and Jeremy.' She passed it to Walsh.

'Sorry if we frightened you two, but we've got some people in there under observation, and I don't want them disturbed, not yet, anyway,' he whispered. 'I want you both to stay here, keep out of sight and don't make a sound. Promise.'

The two frightened youngsters nodded. Jeremy put his arm round Wendy's shoulders and drew her, crouching, into the darkness of a bush. His other hand closed over hers comfortingly. 'We'll stay here, Inspector,' he whispered softly.

Walsh looked down at them, huddled like babes in the wood, and stole away, followed by the other two. He was content to watch and let matters take their course. The white-robed figures within the walls were still on their knees in a circle, their voices low as they made prayers and responses. All seemed harmless enough, so far.

'Inspector, R5. There's another car just coming up,' came the soft voice in the ear-plug receiver.

That was unexpected. Walsh felt the fingers of his hand start drumming, silently, on his thigh. He waited. There was nothing else he could do.

'R5, Inspector. This one's alone and carrying a double-barrelled shotgun. Five eightish, stocky build, coming your way. Any instructions?'

Walsh wriggled round and wormed his way back to the edge of the field, thinking rapidly. He mustn't let the shotgun get as far as the wood. He must assume that it had been brought with the intention of being used, and once within the wood he would not be able to control events. Yet those hedgerows were thin and the fields so open. It would be risky trying to tackle him out there, but there was no real choice.

'R5, follow up on the other side of the hedge. Don't get too close. Reg, follow me, twenty feet behind. Brenda, get in the wood nearest where he'll come if he gets past us,' he breathed into the shielded microphone.

Oblivious to the thorns and flints that pierced his hands and knees, he wormed his way along the hedgerow, keeping only inches from the ground. The hedge was thicker here, where there was a growth of ivy entwined among the brambles. There were soft, rustling sounds of movement coming towards him. The moon was now shrouded by clouds. Through a leafy gap a metallic glint showed momentarily between the leaves, as the gun barrel caught what little light there was. He straightened up and leapt, diving forward over the hedge, his outstretched hands reaching for the shotgun. His right hand found the barrel, and his left, a wrist. He clamped both tight. The person gave a shrill, high-pitched, feminine scream of terror, and tried to pull away, but the weight of his diving body caused them both to fall in a tangled heap. There was a searing blast as one of the barrels went off and a cry of pain from the woman beneath him. Then what breath Walsh had left was forced from his lungs as the watcher flung himself on to the struggling pile of bodies.

It was Finch who loosened the fingers gripping the shotgun and carefully laid it out of harm's way.

Walsh struggled to his feet. That shot had done no injury that he could see.

'Now, who have we got here?' he said, moving round to look at her face.

His answer was a flood of tears.

'I recognize her, boss. It's Mrs Finder,' Reg told him.

'Finder? He's one of those in there, isn't he?' Walsh asked, brushing the dirt and dust from his jacket sleeves.

'That's right. I interviewed him, that's how I came to meet Mrs Finder here.'

'What's the game, Mrs Finder? What brings you out here in the middle of the night with a shotgun?' Walsh asked, still a little bewildered.

'That bloody Alex, that's what. He's been at that bitch Haverston again,' the woman spat out breathlessly, through her convulsive sobbing.

Walsh heard Brenda's call, and turned. There was a group of white-clad figures coming towards him.

'Blast it, put the cuffs on her for good measure,' he said to Reg, and hurried to meet them.

'Dubonis, keep your group together, will you? I don't want them running all over the countryside.'

'That was a shot we heard, wasn't it?' Dubonis cried out in alarm.

'Calm yourself. We have it all in hand. Have you finished here? Good, you can all get yourselves dressed and go home.'

Dubonis looked outraged. 'You've been spying on us, desecrating our service. It's disgraceful. May his wrath fall on your shoulders. You have no right . . .' he spluttered.

Walsh cut him short. 'You've got five minutes to disappear, or else you'll find out what rights I've got,' he replied angrily. 'All except Finder and Haverston, that is. I want them both to come to the station for questioning. Keep an eye on them, Reg. Call in the rest of the troops and see this lot away from here.'

He waited until he had seen Finder and Haverston escorted away, then he remembered Wendy and Jeremy Fry and hastened round the wood. Jeremy had heard him coming and had struggled upright, still supporting the sleepy Wendy, who was rubbing her eyes.

'I think I must have dozed off,' she whispered.

'It's all right now. The others have gone. Come with me, and bring your flowers,' he said, leading the way into the deserted ruin.

He watched as Wendy laid the bunch of flowers and the card down on the cold stone flags.

'Sorry, Martin, but it really wasn't our fault,' she said, wiping a tear from her eye.

'It wasn't, and you have nothing to reproach yourselves for! It's all over now,' Walsh said quietly. 'You'd better get yourselves home. I can arrange a lift for you if you'd rather?'

Jeremy shook his head.

'I think we'll be all right, sir, and thanks, thanks very much. Come Wendy, let's go home.'

'Goodnight, sir,' Wendy said, taking Jeremy's outstretched hand, but looking up at the Inspector's face. 'You really do understand, don't you?'

Walsh lit his pipe, and nodded.

'Off with you, girl,' he said gruffly.

Brenda stood listening, some way behind, and blinked

back a tear of her own. The Chief was a real softy at heart, she thought to herself.

15

'Good grief! You don't mean to tell me you just went off and left your children at home on their own, do you? How many, and how old are they?' Walsh demanded, in the interview room, shaking his head in disbelief.

'There's Jackie, he's twelve, and Samantha, she's ten. They never wake up during the night, they're ever so good,' Mrs Finder replied, defiantly.

'So what if something goes wrong? You don't know, do you?' Walsh stated irritably. 'Brenda, ask the Duty Sergeant to come in, please. So you often go off and leave them, do you?'

'No, of course I don't. I've never done it before. I just didn't know what else to do.'

'Sergeant! Mrs Finder's left her two children at home, unattended. Take her keys and find someone to go and check they're all right, and stay there with them. I don't know when Mrs Finder can go back home, and her husband's still here being questioned,' he said.

The Sergeant went out frowning, wondering who he could send out at this time of night.

'You can't keep me here all night. They'll be frightened if I'm not there when they wake up. You can't do that,' she complained.

'Oh yes, I can, Mrs Finder. You're here for questioning on a possible charge of "Intent to commit Murder". That's very serious. Yes, I can hold you here, all right, and I will do, unless I get some sensible answers to my questions. I can wait until you've got a legal adviser here if you like. You've already been told that,' Walsh said, sternly.

'I haven't got a legal adviser, I just want to go home, please,' she replied anxiously, running her hand through her untidy fair hair. Her face looked pale and drawn with worry, except round her eyes, where the skin was reddened from weeping and rubbing.

'You were out on the night of June twenty-first, weren't you? You followed your husband out to the same wood, didn't you?' Walsh questioned, remorselessly.

The woman frowned, and looked bewildered.

'You've asked me that before and I don't know what you mean. I've never been out there before, never! Honestly I haven't. I don't know why I went up there tonight, really, only I know Alex has been up to his old tricks again, in spite of his promise. I didn't need that nosy old woman round the corner to tell me, and then that fellow Buxton came round and they went off, laughing and joking. It made me feel so mad and angry. It's not like me, honestly. I suddenly got these horrible thoughts going round and round in my mind and I couldn't stop them. Somehow I found myself up in the bedroom holding that damned gun of his, then I was driving the car, only it didn't seem like it was me. I've never been there before, yet I seemed to know just where to go. I just don't know what came over me,' she told them, mumbling, half to herself.

'That was last night. I'm talking about last month. Did you get the same sort of feeling then, when you went out there?' Walsh demanded.

'Last month? You keep on about last month. I don't know what you mean. I've told you, I've never been out there before. Alex has. That's why your man came round to question him. Him and his society meetings! Just an excuse for him to have a romp with that bitch and any of the other old cows there. He promised he wouldn't see her again but he has; that nosy bitch round the corner saw him go into her place. I know men have funny ideas, but last night I just couldn't take it any more, Inspector. Please can I see him. I want to go home. It's all been a nightmare.'

'You wanted to kill him not so very long ago. How do you feel now? Do you still hate him? Do you still want to kill him?' Walsh asked, more sympathetically. She rubbed her eyes again and looked helplessly down at the floor.

'No, that's over. I just want to talk to him. We've had our rows in the past and got over them.' She looked appealingly at him, then buried her face in her hands and sobbed silently.

Walsh looked at Brenda and jerked his head towards the door. 'We'll be back in a minute,' he said.

Outside in the corridor Walsh leaned against the wall, and sniffed.

'Well, what do you think?'

'I'm almost sure that I believe her, Chief. I didn't want to, but I don't think she's got enough up top to have stuck it out as she has. You have been going at her a bit hard.'

Walsh nodded. 'I rather think you might be right. In any case, Finder's car was checked out by Forensic, wasn't it? And her feet are too small. I doubt if she could fake a stride pattern well enough to fool Packstone and his chums.'

He rubbed his stubbly chin thoughtfully. If he freed her and her husband, and if she did then go and kill him, then he, Walsh, was going to look a mighty big fool. On the other hand he couldn't keep them both there indefinitely; besides, in the morning some bright spark of a solicitor was bound to turn up and in a flash her story would be changed. Just gone out with the gun after rabbits, that would be the new line – that and police harassment. Well, he'd have to talk to the husband first, whatever action he took.

'Brenda, you go back with Mrs Finder. I'll have a word with Reg, and Mr Finder.'

It was quite apparent, from the look on Finder's face, that he'd had a really big shock.

'You pushed her too far, didn't you? She was out to get you tonight, to stop your fun and games for good. You do realize that, don't you?' Walsh said, bluntly.

Finder's eyes moved nervously in his weak face.

'I can't understand it. She's never done anything like this before. It ain't like her at all. I wouldn't have gone tonight if I'd realized she felt that strongly about it. Christ, what a mess! What the hell am I going to do now?' he asked, plaintively.

'She wants to talk to you. Do you want to talk to her?'

'I suppose I'd better, hadn't I?'

'That's up to you. You must do what you think is best. All I know is that you've put her through hell tonight. Maybe you owe it to her for doing that,' Walsh suggested.

'Let me see her then,' Finder said, getting to his feet. Walsh led him back to the other room, and left him there.

The elation Walsh had felt earlier, out there by the hedgerow, as he had dived for that gun, had long since dispersed. Now he felt tired and irritable. All that activity had been over nothing more than a stupid, petty, domestic quarrel, and he was no further forward in finding the murderer of Trent, or the missing girl, Joanna Silvers. His fists clenched in frustration. It was almost as if the whole thing had been the result of one of Hera Dubonis's evil spirits getting into a downtrodden housewife and filling her full of a cold-blooded, murderous intent to kill. Dubonis had raised a curse on him, too. He shook his head to dispel those thoughts. They were utter nonsense. Reg was looking at him strangely.

'Are you all right, boss?' Reg asked.

'Of course I am,' he snapped, irritably. 'I've got a bit of a headache, that's all. I don't doubt we're all a bit tired.'

Brenda came out of the interview room. 'They seem to be making up all right, Chief,' she said, as she flicked the unruly lock of hair off her forehead.

'You reckon it's safe to let them go?'

'I think so. She's given him a hell of a fright. He's treating her with a bit of respect in there, probably for the first time in years,' she replied, confidently.

Walsh thought for a moment. 'All right then, I'll leave them to you. Get someone to run them home, then come and join us for a cup of coffee before you go off. Reg's buying. It's too late to be thinking of going to bed.'

He put two spoonfuls of sugar into the steaming mug of nearly black coffee and stirred it vigorously. At just after five in the morning the canteen was almost deserted, and there was an untidy scattering of discarded newspapers and empty crisp packets. The state of the ash trays made one wonder if the concerted anti-smoking campaigns had had any effect at all.

'That's all settled, Chief,' Brenda said, pulling up a chair. 'What are you going to do about her? Are you going to charge her?' she asked.

'Mrs Finder, you mean?' Walsh replied, drawn out of his private reverie. 'I don't know yet. We can get a welfare report on her, and have a word with her doctor. Maybe a psychiatric report as well. If there's nothing serious, I can always read her the riot act, and tell her we're keeping an eye on her.'

'We don't seem to have moved the Trent case forward at all. That's a pity,' Reg added.

'True, although I've got a funny feeling bugging me.

Something just isn't right, but I can't quite get it. Well, we've got another day ahead of us. You're going out with the archaeological team this morning, Reg, aren't you? I think you've wangled better than either of us two. I'm for a wash and brush up. See you both later,' Walsh said, getting up from the table.

16

'Pleased to meet you,' Reginald Finch said to the short, slim, dark-haired man in his early thirties, dressed in well washed blue jeans and a short matching jacket. This was the archaeologist, Graham Franklin, who was to be in charge of the excavations.

'And this is James Head, from the College estate management department,' continued Professor Hughes, indicating a tall, sad-looking man, in a lightweight brown suit and green tie.

'Nice to meet you,' Finch remarked politely.

'Detective Sergeant Finch has been involved in the police investigations concerned with that unfortunate incident at the old Priory, last month. He happens to have an interest in archaeology, so I've invited him along so that he can see for himself what we're doing,' the professor added, rewarding them each with a beaming smile.

'Ah, here comes Mr Privet, he's the farmer here,' Head said, looking across the farmyard toward the red brick Victorian house with its typical slate roof, sash windows and tall chimneys. The farmer was a burly, bald man, in his fifties, a little under six feet tall. In spite of the heat he wore a sleeveless sweater and wellington boots.

'Hello, Mr Head. What's all this, a deputation or something?' His face creased into a grin as he walked round a heap of sand and gravel.

'No, nothing like that,' replied the sad Mr Head. 'This is Professor Hughes, Dr Franklin and Detective Sergeant Finch.'

'What can I do for you, gentlemen?' Privet enquired.

'Well, we've come to tell you that the College wants to do some exploratory excavations on the old Priory site,' Head explained.

'What, that old place! There ain't hardly nothing left there. When d'you want to start and how long'll you be?' It's winter wheat in them fields and I'll want to plough and sow in the next two or three weeks,' he said, seriously.

'They want to start today, Mr Privet. There is that clause in the tenancy agreement giving them the right of access to any site, you know,' Head said, gloomily.

'I know that,' Privet snapped angrily, 'but I think it's bloody bad manners not to give me a decent warning.' He swung his foot and gave a large lump of dried mud a hefty kick that sent it flying across the concrete yard.

Head gave the professor a reproachful look, but Hughes apparently found the passing of a white puffy ball of cloud, trailing smeary tails of thin gossamer high above in the deep blue of the summer sky, of more import than the conversation.

'Sorry about that. Seems there was a slip up in the paperwork. I didn't know myself until yesterday afternoon, just before I rang you,' Head explained.

'How many are you having up there? I don't want hordes of people running around smashing up the hedges and the like,' Privet growled.

'You've no need to worry, Mr Privet. The excavation will be under the control of Dr Franklin here. It'll be a hand dig – shovels and spades, no mechanical assistance, the site's too small for that anyway, and it'll all be self-contained. There'll be a canvas portable loo, and a tent for eating, storage and such like; and a night-watchman, of course. They'll be no inconvenience to you at all. I am right in saying that, aren't I, Dr Franklin?' Head asked.

'Rest assured, any excavation under my control will be carried out efficiently, and with the very minimum of disturbance to yourself, or anyone else. We'll be driving a few exploratory trenches, and depending on what we find we might mount a more comprehensive dig. We shall see. Provided the weather remains fine, it's quite possible that we'll have completed our investigations within three weeks, but you mustn't hold me to that too closely, there are so many variable factors.' Franklin beamed a confident smile at the farmer, who seemed somewhat mollified and impressed by his clipped eloquence.

'Well, in that case I'll let you get on with it then. I'd just like a word before you go, Mr Head, and I wouldn't leave your car there, Sergeant, I'll need the tractor shortly,' he said, nodding towards Finch's car.

'You'd best follow us in your car, Sergeant. We'll go back down the lane, it's not so far to walk to the site then,' Hughes said. 'At least, with our watchman there you won't need to have your patrols come by during the night, will you? My thanks to you, Mr Head, and to you, Mr Privet. No doubt we shall meet again.' The professor moved away towards the parked cars.

Finch did a three-point-turn in the yard and followed Dr Franklin's Range Rover back down the dusty lane.

Head looked as though he were getting an earful, judging from the way the farmer's right fist was thudding emphatically into his open left hand.

The professor led the way out across the field, with a

bouncy, jaunty stride. Franklin grinned, and fell into step with Finch, behind.

'The farmer didn't look too pleased,' Finch said, conversationally.

'They're all like that. I've seen Spanish farmers, Turkish ones, Greek ones, dozens of them, and they all react in the same way. It must be the latent conservatism in their mental attitudes. You've got to talk to them as though you were the local laird. They seem to love that, it works almost every time. Mind you, you can understand the Professor not wanting to let too many people know what we're really looking for. I hope we find something for him. He's going to be awfully disappointed if we don't, and I'm afraid the chances are just about zilch,' Franklin confessed.

'By the way,' Finch remarked, 'when our fellows were searching through the field over the other side of the hill, I had them pick up anything that looked interesting. I've sifted out most of the rubbish. Perhaps you might like to cast your eye over what's left.'

'Sure! What have you got?' Franklin asked.

Finch pulled a small plastic bag out of his pocket and passed it over to Franklin, who dug his hand in and brought out a few of the pieces.

'Roman tile, most of these red bits, but that's Victorian pottery,' he said, flicking out a small white shard with faint blue lines on it. He dug his hand in the bag again. 'More of the same, but this might just be part of a hand axe.' He held up a piece of flint, about two inches long, jagged on one edge, but smooth and gently tapering on the others.

'You see, it's got this bluey white patina, except on the broken bit. That's been formed over the years it's been lying in the ground. Neolithic – New Stone Age. It would have been about that long, originally,' he remarked, holding his hands about eight or nine inches apart. 'Interesting, the Roman tiles. There's no indication of a Roman villa round here. An exposed hill would be an unlikely place, but on the other hand, the Romans could have had a watch tower or signal station up there. Interesting.' He handed the bag back to Finch. 'It's one of the things you can never tell about a site like this, until you dig – just how long it has been occupied. Generally speaking, any hill site with a good defensive position will show some signs of occupation. Here, up on the chalkland, we're not too far away from the Icknield Way and one must remember that these old routes didn't stop being used just because the Romans came and built new roads. The indigenous population would have carried on using them for a long time.'

'You said "indigenous population", not "the Celts". Why?' Finch interposed.

'That's right. The word "Celts" does get used to describe the population of Britain when the Romans arrived, and then there's an implication that they all got driven up north into Scotland or into the mountains of Wales. The Celts were invaders, originating from southern Russia, about six to eight hundred BC, but there were people living here when they arrived. The Celts would have used them as their slaves or serfs and became the ruling military class, just as the Normans did with the Saxon English, when they came over. The Celts were a tall race of people with fair, slightly reddish hair and blue eyes, but most of the population here then were of shorter, wiry stature, with dark hair and brown eyes. So you see, the races were all mixed up when the Romans arrived. Now the word "Celt" is used to describe the black-haired Welsh, who were probably even older inhabitants. Still, that's a whole study in itself, the movement and mixture of populations, I mean,' Franklin added, as they neared the wood on the hill.

Several people, both male and female, came forward to meet them and Finch saw that there was already quite a pile of equipment lying on the stubble field, much of it carried on a half dozen or so wheelbarrows.

'Right then, we might as well get started. Get the mess tent up first. There's room over there if you clear those nettles and brambles, and the loo can go here. When you've done that I'll tell you what to do next,' Franklin instructed busily.

A tall blond young man wearing shorts detached himself from the rest and came over. 'It doesn't need all of us to do that, Dr Franklin. We can start clearing the site if you like.' He held up a spade in his right hand, an action that made his powerful muscles ripple under the golden tan of his skin.

'If you like, Fergusson. It's the chapel I want us to start on. Come, I'll show you.' Franklin led the way into the cool of the shady wood, followed by the professor, Finch and the young, fair-haired giant.

'This won't take long to clear,' Franklin said, looking round the rectangle within the low ivy-covered walls. 'It's surprising that so many of the stone flags have survived the centuries of folk scavenging for building material. Mind you, we did come across a reference, in the sixteenth century, to a ghostly monk who seems to have manifested himself to some of the local population,' he said with a grin. 'Probably they'd had too much of the local beer.'

'Right, Dr Franklin. We'll get started in here. Where will the trenches go?'

'We don't want to pull down any of the trees if we can help, so we might as well take them out from the sides, say here and here,' he said, pointing with his finger. 'Two on either side, and one each from the narrow sides. About twenty foot long. That should enable us to draw up a decent ground plan. Watch out for the water well, though. I don't want anyone disappearing down a fifty-foot hole,' he warned, laughing, as though that would be quite a funny thing to happen.

'We'll run the debris out that way then, and put it over there,' Fergusson suggested.

'Yes, but keep it off the field if you can. Don't want the farmer to have any more to complain about than necessary.'

Fergusson nodded and went off.

Franklin turned to Professor Hughes. 'I plan to concentrate within the walls of the chapel, here. Tomorrow, when the ground's been cleared, we'll remove the stone floor and systematically excavate down to the base level, which won't be difficult to identify since it'll probably be solid chalk. If we don't find your lead box in here, hopefully our exploratory trenches will enable us to identify the Prior's lodging and the other places it might be. Don't get too optimistic, Professor, the chances of a major discovery on a site these days are very, very low, but it's a good opportunity to give the students some practical experience in methodical working and logical interpretation. I doubt if we'll be able to add much to the knowledge of the construction of the religious buildings of that period. Still, you never know what will turn up, that's the exciting thing about it.'

Finch walked back to the car with the professor, leaving Dr Franklin to carry on with the direction of the site activity.

'I know I shouldn't be so excited about this excavation, but I am. Silly, isn't it?' the Professor said, wiping his perspiring brow with a large white handkerchief. He looked incongruous in his surroundings, dressed in brown corduroy trousers and a bright green velvet waistcoat.

'I can understand how you feel. At least you know something was put there once,' Finch remarked, sympathetically.

'You saw our night-watchman, yesterday, I believe.'

'That's right, I did. He's been given one of our radios. He can call into the station if anything worries him, unless he falls asleep, of course. We had a bit of excitement up here last night, you know. The Satanists had another service to exorcise their "spirits of evil". I thought that Satan was responsible for all that evil stuff, but it appears he has rivals. The Chief Inspector wasn't too pleased, we lost a whole night's sleep because of them,' Finch replied, while digging in his pocket for his car keys.

'Give my regards to the Inspector. I hope he'll find time to come up and see the excavation. I'll be here tomorrow. I want to see what's under the floors. Oh dear, that farmer's coming this way. I think I'll be a coward and get in my car, he's a lot bigger than me. In fact, most people are, aren't they? Except round the middle,' he chuckled.

17

'He's just disappeared, Inspector. I know he has,' Hera Dubonis said, wiping a tear from her reddened eyes, smudging her dark make-up even more.

'Come now, Mrs Dubonis, tell me from the beginning. When did you last see him?' Walsh asked, patiently.

'He went off to his office this morning, at a quarter to eight, just like he always does, but they haven't seen him,' she told him.

'But it's only one o'clock now, Mrs Dubonis. How on earth can you say he's disappeared? Surely he must have gone somewhere on business. I can't start a nationwide search just like that, you know. Why don't you go back home and wait? The chances are he'll turn up later on, even if he's not already there waiting for you.'

'You don't understand. I know. Something's wrong. I know it.'

'Now, Mrs Dubonis, you're tired probably. It's easy to start imagining things,' he said firmly.

'You still don't understand. I have the gift. I know things like this; besides, he was so upset last night. Neither of us got much sleep.'

'Why? You had your ceremony, so you've made your peace with whatever it is.'

'You just don't understand, we didn't get that feeling that our worship had been accepted. Walter was so upset, then there was that gun going off and all that with that silly woman. Walter's responsible for getting things right, you see, and these last few months things really haven't gone at all well. It's not been his fault, but he's been worried, and so have I. I'm afraid he might do something silly,' she admitted, looking up at him with fear in her eyes.

'You mean, he might commit suicide, just because things hadn't been quite right for him? That sounds a bit far-fetched. He's a hard-headed businessman, very shrewd. I think you're worrying unduly, Mrs Dubonis. I don't think he's the type.'

'You're so wrong,' she replied, earnestly. 'You just don't understand how the power works or how strong it is. It works from inside the mind, Inspector. Please do something, I'm afraid dreadful things might happen.'

Walsh rubbed his chin thoughtfully. Her anxiety was obviously genuine, nevertheless he wasn't going to be pressured into over-reacting, but he couldn't ignore her entirely.

'I'll see what I can do. You say you've rung round the most likely places. What about his secretary in the office, have you asked her to do some phoning?'

Mrs Dubonis shook her head. 'No, I only said I wanted to contact him. I didn't want to make too much fuss, we don't like his employees getting involved in our private lives.'

'Well, I think we'll have to, and didn't you say that you've got a holiday place somewhere?'

'Yes, we've got a cottage at Brancaster, on the Norfolk coast, but it's not on the phone. We wanted somewhere where we could get away and be left in peace.'

'Ah, well. The chances are that he's gone down there. People sometimes need time on their own while they sort their problems out. He didn't take any clothes with him, did he?'

'No, but we've got all we need in the cottage. He wouldn't need to take anything with him. I do hope you're right. I feel better having talked to you, Inspector. I'll go back home and wait. You'll let me know straight away when you hear something, won't you.'

'Of course I will. Try not to worry unduly,' Walsh replied, getting up from behind his desk to go and open the office door for her.

'Reg, will you deal with that? Get Dubonis's secretary to phone round their customers, and ring Myres at the King's Lynn police station. Ask him if he'll kindly get one of his patrols to check out this cottage in Brancaster; then find out how Packstone's getting on with that metal detector the search teams found in Tomkins's house. Now then, Brenda, you'd started to tell me about Mr Houndell when Mrs Dubonis arrived.'

'That's right, Chief. You remember, Mr Houndell's the

father of that little girl, Gillian, the one that Dubonis took up to the priory the night Trent was killed. We thought he was working on the oil rigs off Aberdeen, but he'd left there three months ago. Well, he's turned up working as a driver for a firm in Oldham. We've just had a report come in from the Force up there. They've interviewed him. Normally he's on local deliveries in and around the Manchester area, but on the nineteenth of June he was loaded up for a run down to Ramsgate. He left early in the morning the next day, but his route took him from the A1 across to pick up the M11 here at Cambridge, where he had a break. He says he slept in his cab whilst he was parked at that big transport café, out towards Babraham. Chief, that's only a few miles away from where Trent was killed,' she said, excitedly.

'Hell, Brenda, come off it. We needed to know where he was because he'd got a good reason to be upset at the Satanists using his daughter. So he was in the area; now the big question is, could he possibly have learned about what his ex-wife and his daughter were up to? It's no good getting excited until we've found a link,' Walsh snapped, testily, rubbing his tired eyes.

'That's right, but I'm coming to that. It seems he went to visit his ex-mother-in-law, Chief, and she could have told him,' Brenda replied, quite unconcerned at his outburst.

'Well, why didn't you say so? That's more like it. What's his shoe size?'

'Nine and a half, that's even better, isn't it? I've already sent Policewoman Knot round to talk to the mother-in-law. We might just have a probable on our hands after all,' she said, smiling broadly.

'Good, well done. Let's hope you're right. After last night's messing about we deserve a bit of luck. Although it's not luck, is it? It's the result of the dogged pursuance of enquiries. We won't be pushing our luck too much if we celebrate with a cup of coffee, will we?' he asked. 'No, don't go yourself, get someone else to fetch it. I need an aspirin as well. I've got a rotten headache.'

'I'm sorry, Chief. I've got some in my bag. I'll get you a glass of water. Won't be a minute,' she said sympathetically. When she came back she found Walsh stretched out on one of the two easy chairs with his feet up on the other. A stack of files and reports lay on the low coffee table beside him.

'Good idea, Chief. You might as well work in comfort.' She put two of the tablets in the glass and stood it within his reach. 'Wait till they've dissolved before you take them. Don't forget you've got Mr and Mrs Finder coming in half an hour,' Brenda fussed.

'Bring them up when they arrive, love,' he replied with a smile.

Walsh drank the dissolved aspirin and grimaced at the bitter taste, thankful that he could wash it away with hot coffee. He looked at the pile of files. There were several cases there. He liked to review them all at least once a week, but the thickest one was the Trent file. He picked it up and weighed it in his hand. It was full of facts, Packstone's facts, meticulously building up the movements of over a dozen people, on that night when the Satanists had had their first midnight revelry and Trent and the girl Joanna had turned up. She, never to be seen again, and he, to lose his young life, having barely achieved maturity. There were interview reports of the individuals concerned, each with attached notes that emphasized the points that were confirmed by other statements. With all the cross-referencing and checking, some of the sheets looked as though a child of three had been given different coloured pens to play with. Then there were Summary sheets, negative ones and positive ones; all the evidence that was positive and provable; and the lists of unconfirmed statements, each cross-referenced to 'Action Taken' reports.

Walsh sighed. Just browsing through it now was a task in itself. Facts confirmed, facts unconfirmed that might not be facts at all, but lies or red herrings, or just nothing to do with the case. It was like trying to do two or three mixed-up jigsaws, with no picture to help. Hunches might cut corners and fit pieces together, but preconceived ideas just caused confusion. Nevertheless, there had been that thought he'd had last night, that something was out of place, or not right – something he should have expected perhaps, but was missing. That same fleeting thought had recurred again this morning, while Reg Finch had been chatting about his visit to the priory site, and had mentioned the ghost of a monk having been seen there once, a long time ago, when some of the locals had been dipping into their cups a bit too deeply. He sighed again. There was no point in straining his mind. He picked up another case file, and started to read.

'Mr and Mrs Finder, Chief Inspector,' Brenda announced, from the open doorway. Walsh heaved himself to his feet. His headache had gone.

'Come in and sit down,' he said, indicating the upright chairs on the other side of his desk.

Brenda closed the door and went to stand over by the window, a slim figure in her tight-fitting jeans and thin white cotton blouse.

Mrs Finder had made a better job of her paintwork this morning; now she looked passably attractive.

'Well, have you settled your differences and got your problems sorted out?' he asked, as he lowered himself into his chair behind the desk.

'Yes, Chief Inspector. I'm ever so sorry for what I did last night. It won't happen again, I promise,' Mrs Finder said, earnestly.

'What about you, Mr Finder?' Walsh inquired, looking directly at the weak face of her husband.

'I'm sorry too. I've told her I'm getting out of that sect of Dubonis's. I shan't go there again, or have anything more to do with any of them again. She's right, they're trouble, and we don't want any more of that,' he said emphatically, as though at that moment at least, he meant it.

'You both realize there are several charges I could bring against Mrs Finder, don't you?' he said sternly. The two of them nodded.

'Well, I'm just going to give you a warning, on this occasion. There're plenty of other ways of sorting out your differences, without the need for violence, or the need to neglect the safety of your family. But be warned, we'll be keeping an eye on you both. If either of you steps out of line again, then I'll throw the book at you. Have you got that? Do you understand what I mean?'

'Oh yes, sir. We do, and thank you, ever so much. We won't give you any trouble again. Will we, Alex?' Mrs Finder said, thankfully.

Her husband nodded, relief showing clearly on his face.

'Right then, you can both go. Remember, I've got my eye on the pair of you.'

Brenda moved over to open the door and let the two Finders out, still murmuring their thanks. 'What was all that about Tomkins having a metal detector, Chief? I thought we'd well and truly eliminated him from the Trent case,' she asked with a frown.

'We probably have, but the search found a metal detector in his garage, so we've got to have it checked. Tomkins says he's had it for years, but it's the same make as

Trent's. Did Reg tell you he'd found that Tomkins's cousin in London did time for robbery some years ago? We think Tomkins has been getting rid of his loot through him. It'd be nice to tie it all up so neatly,' Walsh replied, hopefully.

Reg Finch came hurrying in, without knocking. 'Boss,' he said, breathing heavily, having run up the stairs, 'I've got Myres on the phone from Norfolk. I've told them to transfer the call up here. They've found Dubonis, in that cottage of theirs. He's gone and hung himself from a hook in a beam in the kitchen. He's dead, boss.'

18

'I'm so very sorry, Mrs Dubonis,' Walsh said sympathetically, looking down at the woman on the settee, sobbing, with her face buried in her hands. 'You were quite right when you said you had the feeling something was wrong,' he added, hoping to distract her mind. Her grief was certainly genuine.

'I told you I had the power, didn't I?' she said, raising her head and looking up at him. 'Poor Walter. He wouldn't have been able to help himself. Once he decides to get into your mind there is nothing you can do to stop him. There must be some very strong power out there at the old priory, to have upset him like this. Usually there's an even balance between good and evil at these old chapels, but not there. Whatever it is, it made him angry, that's why that poor young man died, and then he brought Mrs Finder out there with that shotgun. She was meant to kill, but you thwarted him and prevented that, Inspector. Take special care, he might want revenge on you for that. I can't tell at the moment, I'm too upset.'

'You say young Trent had to die. Why? And what about the girl who was with him? What would have happened to her?' Walsh asked.

'Someone else must have been watching us, besides Trent and his girl. Someone receptive to him, so he took the boy. The girl, I don't know. He wouldn't have wanted her just then, later perhaps, but not having just taken the boy. I think she may have suffered grievously, and all because we went to the wrong place. How could we have known? We should have kept to the places we knew and not gone out there. Now poor Walter's been made to pay for our mistakes, and I'm left here alone. I can't run the sect. I'm just a woman, and I feel so helpless, watching all the things that happen, but unable to do anything about them.'

'Have you got anyone who can come and stay with you, Mrs Dubonis? You oughtn't to be on your own,' he asked.

Mrs Dubonis wiped her eyes again, with her wet handkerchief. 'I'll ask my sister to come over. She lives in Ely, so it's not far. I'll do that now, if you'll pass me the phone.'

Walsh did as he was asked, and listened to the conversation. 'I've brought a young policewoman with me. She can sit with you until your sister arrives.' He opened the sitting-room door and beckoned her in.

'Perhaps you could make Mrs Dubonis a good strong cup of tea or coffee while you're waiting. Report to the Duty Sergeant when you get back. You'll let me know if there's anything I can do to help, won't you, Mrs Dubonis?' he said, as he left.

'This suicide's a nasty business. It's incredible that a man like Dubonis would do such a thing. Do you think he did it? Killed Trent, I mean, Sidney?' the Chief Constable asked thoughtfully, leaning forward on the tooled leather top of his large mahogany desk.

'If he did, I can't for the life of me work out how he managed it. His wife is convinced that he had offended the Devil, and that the Devil got into his mind as a punishment. I'm serious, she really believes it. In our language it would be described as "extreme depression resulting from a series of confidence-destroying events", or the Coroner's phrase, "Suicide, while the balance of the mind was disturbed". In Mrs Dubonis's case, she thinks the Devil moved in and disturbed the balance. She says these things so confidently that, given half a chance, you'd almost believe her,' Walsh replied.

The CC nodded. 'And this Mrs Finder, you've let her off? Do you think that was wise?'

'Well, yes. There's nothing from the Welfare people and her doctor to suggest she's got a screw loose. Her husband's more the problem; if there's a woman about it seems he has difficulty keeping his trousers done up, but I've given them a bit of a fright. I really can't see that there was anything to gain by charging her; in fact, it might have made things worse.'

Once again the Chief Constable nodded. 'What are you going to do about this lorry driver fellow, the father of the little girl?' he asked.

'If I find that he could have known what his ex-wife was up to with their daughter, then I'll have him in. Someone's out seeing Mrs Houndell's mother now. It seems she got on better with the son-in-law than her daughter did. Did I tell you that the College archaeological excavation has started on the old priory site? I let Reg Finch go out there this morning, it's just up his street. He reckons that Professor Hughes is getting all excited about the possibilities of finding that old Bible. Pretty slim chance, I'd have thought,' Walsh exclaimed.

The CC nodded yet again, reminding Walsh of one of those nodding ducks that pecks at glasses of water that he had seen when a child

'Are you absolutely sure you can't tie Dubonis up with Trent's death, Sidney? His suicide makes much more sense if you do. In fact, it's the only obvious explanation. I really think you should spend a bit more time on that aspect. Get Packstone to check again on the forensic side. You don't need the kind of evidence that would convince a jury, do you? Just enough to make it look reasonably certain. Then if we do draw a blank on your other suspects we could put the case in limbo, *sine die* so to speak, on the basis that Dubonis was probably the killer and he committed suicide because he thought you were coming too close to being able to prove it.'

'I'll have it looked at again, but I tell you, at the moment I think it's waste of time,' Walsh replied, his expression clearly showing that he did not think much of the implied suggestion that evidence should be presented so that it might support a false hypothesis.

'All right, Sidney. Let's leave it at that for now. You'll let me know if anything important turns up. If not, I'll see you in a couple of days' time.'

Walsh went back to his office. The effect of the aspirins was wearing off and that wretched headache was starting to return again, together with that nagging thought that he'd had last night, the feeling that there was something not quite right with the Trent case, but he could not pin it down into words. He picked up the file of another of his cases and settled down to study it, but the phone rang before he'd turned more than three of the closely written pages.

'Chief, I've got Policewoman Knot with me. She's just

come back from seeing Houndell's ex-mother-in-law. I think you should hear what she has got to say before she types out her report. May I bring her up?' Brenda asked.

'Do that, Brenda,' he replied, wondering if he was ever going to get the time to concentrate on these cases of his.

Policewoman Knot was barely twenty-one and looked younger. 'Sit down. What have you got to tell us?' he said, kindly. There did not seem to be any need to set her at her ease, she looked confident enough as it was.

'Mrs Drydon is her name, sir. She's a widow, aged about sixty-five and quite a sensible woman. It seems she'd always got on well with her daughter's husband and, frankly, she tends to blame her daughter's behaviour for breaking up the marriage by getting into the wrong company. Well, he'd kept in touch, sending birthday and Christmas cards, that sort of thing, and occasionally, if he was this way, he would pop in and have a chat, although he hadn't been round for several months up till then. He called in to see her about ten o'clock the night in question. She thinks he left his lorry parked on a bit of waste ground, just down the road from her house. Anyway, they chatted, and as you'd expect, the conversation got round eventually to her daughter, and what she was up to. He said that he supposed she would be out with those funny people tonight – those are his words, sir – it being the summer solstice, and that he wondered which old church they would be using this time.' She paused to take out her notebook and to refer to something she had written.

'She says that she told him that she thought they were going out to an old priory on the other side of the Gog Magog hills. She guessed that because when the daughter had been round to see her a few days earlier, she'd asked to look at her mother's maps, and that was the area she was looking for. Then Houndell asked who was looking after his daughter, Gillian, because she was usually left with her grandmother when Mrs Houndell was going out anywhere, but Mrs Drydon didn't know where the little girl was, and had to say so. At that, Houndell started to get angry and said that if her mother had taken her to any of her damned orgies, he'd kill her – the mother, that it. Well, Mrs Drydon calmed him down after a while, saying that even her own daughter couldn't be that wicked. Anyway, he stayed for about another hour or so, then asked if he could borrow her Mini for a little while, so that he could pop into town and get something to eat. She told him that it was too late and there wouldn't be any places still open, and she offered to fix him up with a meal, but he didn't want that. In the end she let him have her car keys, and he went off. Mrs Drydon then went to bed. She didn't hear her car come back, but it was there next morning and the keys were lying on the front door mat. He'd put them through the letter-box, just like he'd promised. She hasn't seen or heard from him since. That's it, sir. That's all I could get from her,' she said.

'Well, you seem to have done very well. Thank you very much. Now I'd like you to type up your report and get Mrs Drydon's statement signed. Let me have them as soon as possible. Would you go and do that now, please? Brenda, you'd better stay,' Walsh remarked, thoughtfully, but he sat, staring into space for some moments after Policewoman Knot had left. Then he picked up the phone and dialled a number.

'Richard Packstone, please. It's Inspector Walsh,' he requested of the Forensic department. 'Richard, there's another car to be checked over in the Trent case. It's a Mini. Policewoman Knot will give you the details. She's downstairs somewhere writing up some reports. Yes, we might be on to something concrete this time. Thanks.' He put the phone down. 'What do you think, Brenda?'

'He never mentioned borrowing his ex-mother-in-law's car, not in his statement up in Oldham, he didn't. That's suspicious for a start. What it doesn't explain is why he should have killed Trent and taken Joanna Silvers away. I can understand him being wild about his little girl being taken to a place like that, even if he wasn't a good father in other ways. He doesn't seem to have taken much interest in the girl, never wanting to see her, that is. But on the other hand, we've now got a connection with the old Priory, so he could have been there, therefore he could have done it. If he did, he could have taken Joanna's body away in his lorry. It could be dumped anywhere between here and Ramsgate,' she suggested.

Walsh nodded. 'I think we should facsimile a copy of young Knot's report, and the statement of his ex-mother-in-law, up to Oldham. Let them question him again. If he can't come up with a better story than he has already, then they'll have to hold him on suspicion until one or other of us gets there. We'll have Packstone's report on the Mini by then. Will you see to that for me, please? Now what about the "missing persons", "sex crimes" angle? How's that coming along?' he asked.

Brenda grimaced. 'Dead slow, Chief, it's hard grind. We've only got two people working on it, you know, that's all we can spare at the moment. They weren't even half-way through yesterday when I spoke to them, but I haven't been down there today, yet. They'll shout loud enough if they come up with something, but they've done all those in the local area, and now they're working on the East Anglia groupage. The further away they get, the less likely it is that they'll turn anything up on any of those on our list.'

Walsh scratched his head. 'It's got to be done,' he said.

Left on his own again he carried on working through his files. As he read on, his mind seemed able to replay the conversations of that day and the day before without upsetting his concentration. That was until the feeling that there was something that ought to have happened with this Trent case that hadn't happened, came back into his mind again, and drove all other thoughts away. Now it was clear: twice something ought to have occurred that hadn't. But what was the significance? He pushed the files on the desk away from him and felt for his pipe and tobacco. With his pipe well alight he propped his chin in his hands, leaning forward with his elbows on the desk, and tried to think clearly. Something that hadn't happened that ought to have done. Twice, not just once. It didn't fit in with anything he knew and there could so easily be a satisfactory explanation, but on the other hand? His fertile imagination had no problem in throwing up a variety of suitable scenarios, none of which was supported by any of the facts. Was he indulging in fantasy? These thoughts all had a common factor in the old priory ruins, though, and they explained some things, even if they posed other problems. Nevertheless, there was a certain logic behind them. He looked at his watch, it had just gone half-past four. He picked up the phone.

'Brenda, I want you to do something for me.' He explained what it was that he wanted checked out.

'Yes. OK, Chief. I'll get them working on it right away. It's bit of a long shot, though, isn't it, Chief?' she asked.

'Maybe, Brenda, maybe,' he replied. 'Anyway, I'm going off home now. Ring me at home if you find anything, good or bad. It's important. If you apply logical thinking to that possiblity, then something may well happen out there tonight.'

'Well, you're not leaving me out if there is, Chief, and Reg will think the same,' she replied.

'Don't be silly, girl. I'm only playing a hunch, and it's highly likely it'll be a complete waste of time. Anyway, you lost a whole night's sleep last night.'

'So did you, but we'll see what we come up with first. I'll ring as soon as I know.'

'You do that,' he replied.

19

It was just before seven o'clock when the sound of the telephone roused Walsh from the doze he'd been having in the easy chair in his lounge. A doze disturbed by fleeting visions of ruins, devilish figures, monks, and fragments of illuminated manuscripts.

It was Reg Finch's voice that he heard.

'Boss! That Houndell fellow's done a bolt!' he exclaimed excitedly. 'The Oldham police went after him as soon as they got the facsimile copies of those reports. He wasn't at work, he'd told them that he needed a few days off to sort out private affairs; and he wasn't at his digs either. He told his landlady that there'd been a death in the family, down south somewhere, she couldn't remember where, and he'd got to go to the funeral . . .'

'All right, Reg, don't keep on. So he's bunked. What time did he leave, do they know that? Has a call gone out to pick him up? Is he in a car or on foot? What's he wearing?' Walsh snapped, impatiently.

'He hadn't been gone long, boss. They put a call out straight away. He's driving one of the old-model Rovers, a beige three and a half litre. A Midlands motorway patrol reported that a car of that description passed the Coventry turn-off on the M6 about an hour and a half ago, and an M1 patrol is sure a similar car came off the motorway at junction 16, the Northampton turn-off, about an hour ago. Registration number's not confirmed, of course, but you don't see many of that model still on the road nowadays. With all the patrols alerted, we're bound to get another report in soon, if he's still on the road, that is.'

Walsh hesitated. He couldn't control activity from here, at home, and there were other things going on, as well as this. 'Has Packstone finished doing Mrs Drydon's Mini yet, Reg?' he asked.

'I don't know, but I'll find out, if you like.'

'Do that! I'm coming into HQ, Reg. I'll be with you in ten minutes.'

Walsh put the phone down and wrote a message on the pad for his wife. She wouldn't be surprised if he wasn't there when she got home, he'd hardly seen her at all the past few days. It took him longer than ten minutes, though. Reg Finch looked as tired as he felt himself, Walsh thought.

'How's it going?' he inquired.

Finch looked up at him. 'I'm glad you're here. He's on the A45, coming up to St Neots. A Panda car's spotted him. I've told it to follow, since he appears to be coming this way. I thought you'd want to find out where he's going,' he explained.

Walsh leaned over the desk to look at where Finch's finger was pointing on the map.

'He's there, is he?'

Finch nodded.

'I do want to find out where he's going, but I don't want to risk losing him. I think we'll get mobile and head out that way, ourselves. Where's Brenda?' Walsh wanted to know.

'She was having a kip in your office, half an hour a ago, boss. Reckoned it was going to be an all night job, what you asked her to do. She told the Duty Sergeant to wake her at eight, but the others are working on it in the meantime. Oh yes, and Packstone says they're still working on the stuff from Mrs Drydon's car, in the lab. They'll be several hours yet, but there's nothing positive up to now.'

'Oh! Pity, I was hoping we'd have had some good news. We'd better leave Brenda and do this on our own. Get the car round, will you? I'll meet you outside in a minute.'

'He's turned off into St Neots,' the Panda car driver reported.

'Keep with him,' Walsh instructed, speaking into the black radio handset.

'Put your foot down, Reg, he could be going to ground,' he added, reaching forward to search the dashboard pocket for the St Neots street map.

'Where are you now?' Walsh asked the Panda driver, when the map was spread open on his lap.

'Just turned off the Eynesbury Road, sir, into Marlyn Lane. Ah, now he's going right, that's Hampton Grove. It's bungalows all round here. Hello, he's pulling up. I've been on his tail nearly half an hour now, and I don't think he's spotted me, yet. Yes, he's stopped, he's got out and is going into a bungalow.'

'Good work. Just stay there. We'll be with you in about five minutes,' Walsh informed him.

'Looks as though we've got him nicely cornered, boss,' Finch commented.

*

'He's still in there, sir. He went to the side door,' the Panda driver reported to Walsh.

'Right, let's go and get him. I don't want any violence if we can avoid it, but be ready if he tries to make a break for it. Constable, you stay by the front door, we'll go the way he went, down the side.'

The bungalow was small and semi-detached. The front garden was well cared for, neat, with colourful flower beds round a tiny lawn. A shingle drive led down the side. Walsh pressed the bell and stood back from the glass-paned kitchen door, tensed and alert. He had to ring a second time before it was opened – by a little, grey-haired woman, well into her sixties, leaning on an aluminium walking-frame.

'I'm a police officer,' he said, holding out his identity warrant card for her to see.

She peered at it suspiciously through her spectacles.

'What d'you want?' she asked.

'You've got a Mr Houndell here. I'd like a word with him, if you please.'

There was movement behind the woman, and a short plump man in his forties, with a weak chin and protruding blue eyes, came into the room.

'Anything the matter, Aunt May?' he asked.

The woman turned to him.

'Them's police, they say they want a word with you, Arthur. You ain't been up to mischief, have yer?' She looked at him accusingly.

Houndell frowned and looked mystified. 'What do you want with me then? I ain't been speeding and me car's got an MOT,' he whined.

Walsh frowned as well, this wasn't quite what he had expected. 'It's to do with that matter the police in Oldham saw you about, Mr Houndell. It's important, and you'd gone away from your digs without telling anyone where you were going.'

'So what? They never said I'd got to tell them everything I did. Tough on them, anyway; me Aunt Joan died the other day and I've come to take me Aunt May to the funeral tomorrow, and no bugger's going to stop me, are they, Aunt May?' he said defiantly, but moved so that his aunt stood between himself and the open door.

'No, they ain't, Arthur. You're going to take me. See, mister, he is so. I can't go on the bus, not with me legs, so Arthur's got to take me in his car. I can't miss me sister's funeral, can I? Wouldn't be proper.'

Walsh looked at Houndell's weak chin and his image of a brutal, violent murderer, desperately seeking to escape arrest, faded away completely. And there was no bringing it back, not while looking at the spiritless man in front of him.

'I think we'd better come in and have a talk. We've got some questions to ask. It shouldn't take long,' Walsh said, despondently.

'That was a bloody waste of time, boss,' Finch said later, as he and Walsh walked from the car into HQ. 'I can't say I've ever met anyone less like a murderer than him.'

Walsh just grunted. Finch wasn't right, it wasn't a waste of time. They'd done what they'd had to do. What he really meant was that they'd got all excited that evening thinking they were going to confront Trent's murderer. An attitude of mind created, no doubt, by last night's success with Tomkins, plus two nearly sleepless nights affecting their judgement. That needed rectifying.

'I'll have a word with Brenda and Packstone first, then I'm going home to bed, Reg,' Walsh said.

*

Walsh reached out to turn off the bedside light. As his hand passed over the telephone, it rang. He picked up the receiver.

'Boss, we've found a connection,' came Finch's excited voice.

It took some seconds for Walsh's brain to get working. 'Just a minute, Reg. I asked Brenda to do that. How come you're telling me about it?' Walsh asked.

'Nothing to worry about, boss. We've just been doing a bit of co-operating. I thought I'd give her a hand before I went off,' he replied.

'What have you come up with?'

'It's a Newmarket man, boss. We've dug out the original statements and enquiry reports. It ties up just as you thought it might, boss.'

There was a pause, while Walsh's mind adjusted from the speculative section of his brain to the part that determined positive action. The truth was that he'd been pessimistic about the chances of this particular hunch progressing, and hadn't planned further. So far, this case had been full of good leads that had led nowhere.

'Let me think a minute,' he said, eventually. 'We could just pick him up, now; but he's clever; what if we find nothing at the house? He's had plenty of time to cover his tracks. If we want to tie this up good and proper we've got to catch him red-handed, doing what we think he might do. Maybe there's nothing there, anyway. If there isn't, all we'll have done is waste a few hours. He isn't going to run tonight, so he'll still be there in the morning, and we'll have to hope that Forensic can tie it up. On the other hand, all we've got to do is watch. If he comes, we've got him, and we mustn't forget the night-watchman,' he pondered out loud. 'Right, that settles it. I'm going out there. If you two want to come as well, you can, you're both old enough to look after yourselves.

We've had one wild goose chase tonight so I'm not taking a whole squad out there, too many would be spotted anyway. You'll have to dress for the occasion, we'll have to do some sneaky crawling to get in position. Our friend's got sharp eyes and keen ears. I'll be down at HQ in fifteen minutes, Reg.'

He put the phone down, pushed himself upright off the bed with an effort and went over to his wardrobe. Dark corduroy trousers, they'd do, black socks and plimsolls, a grey shirt – he hadn't got a black one, but it wouldn't matter, the dark, lightweight anorak could be zipped up to the neck – and the black, woolly, fisherman's type hat.

Tight-lipped, Gwen Walsh stood watching her husband dress rapidly.

'It'll be a waste of time, love,' he told her. 'Ninety per cent of these things are. No need to worry about me tonight, though, it seems I've got a couple of bodyguards.'

Her features changed hardly at all. 'What worries me is that you don't seem to realize that you're getting older, you can't do the things you used to do,' she replied.

'You're wrong there, love. I do realize it and I take double the care instead.'

He kissed her lovingly. 'See you later, sweetheart,' he added, as he hurried down the stairs and out to his car. Gwen Walsh shrugged as she heard his car accelerate away. Then she did what she had so often done before: she went to bed with a good book, and eventually fell asleep, with the light still on.

Walsh drove slowly over the rutted surface of the old Roman road, without the help of the car's lights. The sky was dark, overcast; and there was little natural light to see by, just a faint glow above that indicated the whereabouts of the moon on the other side of the clouds. His two companions were quiet, lost in their own thoughts. The engine purred softly at little over tick-over speed. He slipped the clutch and allowed the car to roll down the road under its own impetus. Through the open windows the sound of the tyres on the hard flinty surface seemed loud. It wasn't the kind of noise that would travel far; even so, there was no point in taking any chances. At the bottom of the slope was a tiny copse of slender birch trees and a thick undergrowth of bushes and briers. He ran the car into a gap and switched the engine off.

'We'll go the rest of the way on foot. I reckon it's about three quarters of a mile or so, maybe as much as a mile. We want to come in from the west, away from where the night-watchman will be. Fortunately, what wind there is is in our faces. Ready? Darken up then.' He rubbed the fine soot on his hands and wrists, then, looking in the driving-mirror, on his face as well.

It seemed a bit melodramatic, but it was a sensible thing to do. White faces and hands reflected light and could be seen even in pitch blackness, as a faintly luminous blur. He locked the car and stuffed the keys in the same pocket as his handkerchief, tightly, so that they would not betray his movements by clinking, then led the way, keeping close up into the darkness of the hedgerows, bending low if there was any chance that his silhouette might stand out against a lighter background. It took less than twenty minutes before he could make out the dark mass of the wood on the hill. He paused to let the others catch up. There was a hedgerow leading up the slight slope. The hill was perhaps two hundred yards away.

He turned to his companions. 'We'll do this last bit on hands and knees. When we get there we'll have to play it by ear,' he whispered, softly. 'We don't know which way he'll come in, if he's coming at all, but we know he'll have to nobble the night-watchman first. That's when we've got to grab him, for obvious reasons. I'll get as near as I can to the tent on the right side. Reg, you get close on the left. Brenda, you just get as near as you can. OK?'

He heard grunts of acknowledgement.

Another look round: there was no sign of movement, everything was still. He wriggled through a gap and started crawling. The wild grasses grew long, close up to the hedge, but they were dry now, after the weeks of rainless summer days, and they brushed against his face as he moved forward. He'd started to count, he didn't quite know why. He'd counted four hundred and fifty and he could see the trees more clearly, soaring away above him. A little further on he stopped for a rest; he was starting to breathe heavily and noisily. He allowed himself five minutes, then moved on. Ahead, just inside the wood, there was a strangely regular shape. He approached even more cautiously. It was a fresh pile of weeds, creepers and sods of earth, the soil heap of debris that had been cleared from the site during the day. He crept round the western edge of the trees, a couple of yards or so into the undergrowth. The faint sound of a radio broke the stillness, growing louder as he approached. He could see the outline of the tent, looming up in the darkness. Not a big one, about eight feet square, as well as he could judge. One of the pavilion type, with a canopy at the front. The radio was masking any noise that he might be making, but still he moved with care. There appeared to be a chair in the entrance, a padded sunchair with adjustable arms, and a dark shadow reclining in it. That must be the night-watchman, and he could hear snoring, in spite of the radio.

The undergrowth had been flattened for several feet round the tent, but there was a shrub near by, close to a tree. He backed into the space between them. It was as good a place as he was going to find. The watchman was about ten feet away. He dug his feet into the soft earth to give him a grip if he needed to spring forward, and settled down to wait and watch. There was a slight movement in a bush over the other side of the path from the tent to the ruins. He wondered which one of the other two that was, unless he had imagined it. Watching from this position, so close to the ground, made his neck ache, so he laid his head on the ground and concentrated on listening instead. In spite of his anorak, he started to feel chilly. He tried to ignore the passing of time and the desire to look at his watch, his job was to watch and wait; there was nothing else to do, except think. He could be making a fool of himself, here. It was one of those occasions when the results alone would justify the action.

The man in the chair grunted and changed his position. Walsh's ears could now distinguish between some of the sounds other than the radio, mostly the rustling of the leaves in the branches around and above him. He flexed his stiffening muscles, trying to get some warmth into them. How long had he been lying there? An hour, an hour and a half perhaps. Time was dragging. He needed some new thoughts to occupy a mind that was starting to complain at inactivity. The ear nearest the ground detected a different sound, a faint hum. A plane? No, that would be his other ear. A vehicle, then? A slow-revving engine? It was certainly a low-pitched throb. He brought his head up, turning it slowly from side to side, trying to focus on the sound to get the direction, but the radio swamped it. He put his ear to the ground again, but now there was nothing, nothing at all. Maybe he was overstretching his senses and imagining things. On the other hand, although the expected visitor would hardly be likely to drive right up to the site, for that would be too risky, he would need transport later. Maybe he would drive up as close as he dared, then move on foot. The sky had lightened just a fraction. The clouds were still unbroken, but they must be getting thinner. He tried to estimate the time again, possibly it was around one o'clock. He moved his body slightly, he felt cold and stiff, but his new position wasn't as comfortable as the old one. He needed to maintain his vigilance now. This was the danger point, the time when enthusiasm was waning and doubts would take over a mind that still needed feeding with positive thoughts.

This person he was waiting for, what was his real character like? Patient, clever, but one that could get carried away at moments of emotional stress. He was introverted too, that was dangerous. Such people's thoughts ranged into fantasy, sometimes.

His ears picked up the faintest of rustles, just a fraction too long to fit into the pattern of sounds his hearing had become accustomed to. He sensed rather than saw the darker than darkness of a shadow on the beaten path. He held his breath as his heart beat faster and the adrenalin rushed into his blood. The shadow moved nearer, making no sound that rose above the level of the music from the radio. The shadow became a man, standing, looking down at the sleeping figure sprawled in the chair. Slowly the man raised his right arm, and Walsh's eyes received a burst of animal power, revealing the blur in the man's hand as a hammer. He leapt forward desperately, his right hand outstretched to grab it, before it descended on the innocent head of the sleeping night-watchman.

20

The dark figure was very quick, reacting instantly to Walsh's attack. He countered by bringing his arm down in a vicious backhand sweep, one that would have brought forth appreciative cries on the Centre Court at Wimbledon. The heavy hammer thudded into Walsh's shoulder, sending him reeling to the ground. The figure continued to turn on nimble feet, to meet Finch's approach. His right arm gained speed again, and the hammer whammed into the pit of Finch's stomach. Finch doubled up with an agonized gasp, and stumbled into the garden chair, sending the night-watchman crashing to the ground. Walsh's eyes blazed in frustrated anger as he scrabbled forward on hands and knees, desperately trying to grapple the man's legs, then reeled hurriedly aside to avoid a savage kick at his face. The man with the hammer hesitated for a brief moment and decided the odds against him were too great. He turned, and ran back the way he had come. A slighter figure darted out of the undergrowth ahead of him, as Walsh scrambled to his feet and pounded after them, out of the wood, into the open field. In the faint light he could see the shape of a Land Rover, some fifty or so yards away, by the hedge. The first, slimmer, figure, which had gained ground on the second, wrenched at the driver's door, reached in and grabbed something shiny, then disappeared round the back of the vehicle.

The burly man abruptly changed direction and headed across the field, with a fast, loping stride.

Breathing heavily between clenched teeth, Walsh

sprinted after him, trying to ignore the pain in his right shoulder, but the man in front was faster and getting away from him. He heard the roar of the Land Rover engine and saw the sweep of the headlights across the field as the vehicle swung round.

The man ahead leaped through a gap in the far hedge and was lost to sight for a moment. The Land Rover was making for the lane. Brenda would have guessed the burly man's intentions and was trying to get there first. Finch was way behind, so it was up to Walsh to keep the man in sight. He stumbled, gasping, after his quarry, through that hedge, across another stubble field and another hedge, where brambles tore and ripped his clothes. The quarry turned and looked back, then disappeared through an open gate. Where the Land Rover was now, Walsh could not tell, all he could hear was the pounding of blood in his ears. Through that gate and a swerve to the right, on to the track leading to the farmhouse, easier going, but the other man was far ahead and still running strongly.

Walsh staggered on after him. The Land Rover came roaring up behind him, its horn blared urgently. Walsh lurched to one side. The vehicle brushed his shoulder as it sped past with headlights blazing. It was gaining rapidly on the running man, who was now sprinting desperately, across the yard, to the farmhouse. For a fleeting moment Walsh thought the man would be run down but he made it to the front door and disappeared inside. The Land Rover screeched to a halt. Brenda leapt out and ran round to the side of the building. Walsh kept straight on, his eyes fixed on that front door, his breath rasping in his throat and his mind numbed by the sheer effort of keeping moving.

He heard the smash of breaking glass in an upper window and the scream of warning from Brenda in the shadows, but it was instinct, not reason, that caused him, at the last moment, to dive to one side. The blast of a gun shattered the night air, and a hail of lead shot tore at the ground beside him. A second blast of the gun scattered concrete dust, harmlessly, behind him, as he gave another convulsive leap to his right and scuttled on hands and feet like a frightened crab, to safety.

'Are you all right, Chief?' Brenda whispered anxiously, as he lay there, gasping for breath.

'Just about,' he groaned, pushing himself to his knees.

'Well, you certainly like to live dangerously,' she remarked, disapprovingly.

'Just call up some reinforcements, will you?' he snapped, suddenly aware of his suicidal folly in making such a direct approach to a cornered killer. The warning from Hera Dubonis, that the Devil had him down as a marked man, flashed through his mind. He'd already had a few narrow escapes, too many, and too close for comfort. He put the thought out of his mind.

'They're already on their way, Chief. I radioed in while I was in the Land Rover. Reg wasn't far behind you, he went round the back. I hope he's all right.'

Walsh unzipped his anorak and pulled out his own radio phone.

'Reg, where are you?'

'Round the back of the house, over the far side from you, boss. There's a back door and french windows, but he can't get out without our seeing him.' Reg's voice was strained and hoarse.

There was another shot, muffled, from the other side of the building.

'Come on, girl, while he's at the back of the house. We'll be safer over there!' Walsh grabbed Brenda's arm, and they ran over to the corner of the tractor shed.

'He must have caught a glimpse of me, boss, but I'm all right where I am,' Finch reported over the radio.

'Stick where you are, Reg. I'm changing frequency to find out where our help is.'

Walsh punched some buttons on the radio phone. 'HQ, HQ, Walsh speaking. Where's our help? We've got this chap holed up in the farmhouse, and he's armed.'

After a momentary pause, he heard the Duty Officer's voice. 'The first car will be with you in a couple of minutes or so, sir. The second car's a few minutes behind that, but it's got two marksmen with rifles, some hand-guns and the emergency gear. Would you change to frequency twenty-five, please? I've got the cars on that, and the Chief Constable would like a word with you as well. He's at his home.'

'Right, I'll ring him just as soon as I've got the house properly surrounded.'

Walsh changed the frequency.

'Walsh to cars. Suspect is holed up in the farmhouse, armed with a shotgun. Come up the lane and stop behind the Land Rover in the farmyard. I want a rifle front and rear, hand-guns each side, and some spotlights round the back. Half of you work your way round the east side. Reg Finch's there, he'll home you in. I'm at the corner of the tractor shed, on the west side. Bring me a hand-gun and a megaphone.'

He saw car lights approaching, far up the lane. The house was quiet, there was no sign of movement for the moment. He dialled the Chief Constable's number.

'Walsh here, sir. We've got the fellow trapped in the farmhouse. We'll have the place properly surrounded in a few moments, but he can't get out,' he said, confidently.

'What fellow?'

'Privet, the farmer.'

'Is there a hostage? Don't you do anything rash.'

'No sign of one. It's a straightforward siege situation now. When I get a megaphone I'll start talking to him.'

'I'm coming to see for myself,' the CC said, and rang off.

Walsh shrugged, then was startled by a sudden flurry of shots and shouts from the other side of the house. 'What the hell's going on, Reg?' he yelled anxiously into the radio.

'He tried to get out through the back door, boss, and fired two shots. Didn't hit anyone though. He bolted back inside when I called on him to drop his gun or we'd shoot. We've got the lights rigged up now. He's back upstairs again, I think.'

'Don't take any risks, Reg,' Walsh ordered, then set about checking the disposition of his men round the farmhouse. There was little chance now for Privet to break through that cordon, even with a couple of blasts from his shotgun, and it was unlikely that he could make good an escape, if he did. Several more shots had been fired, seemingly at random, as Walsh had made his way carefully round the house, but they had come from the upper floor, where Privet presumably felt safer.

Walsh sat on the front wheel of a tractor, the megaphone held in his hand. He was well out of shotgun range, but with a clear view of the well-lit front of the house. There had been no further movement for some time, except an occasional flash from behind the upper windows, as the lights caught what appeared to be the barrel of the gun. No doubt Privet was prowling round the upstairs rooms like a tiger round a cage, looking for some way out. Twice now, Walsh had used the megaphone to tell Privet that he was surrounded, that there was no possibility of escape, and that he should throw the shotgun out of the window and come out himself, with his hands held high above his head; but there had been no response to either invitation, just silence. It would take time for Privet's mind to come to terms with the reality of the situation.

Well, now they'd all got plenty of time to think and ponder, there was no need for any panic measures.

Walsh rubbed his tired eyes, and then the shoulder that had taken Privet's hammer blow, reminding himself again of the failure of his original ambush. That plan had seemed to be so safe and sound then. He'd been over-confident, perhaps, but a set up like that, in the dark, relying on surprise against an unknown quantity, was bound to carry a high degree of risk. He'd been damned lucky though, that it had turned out as well as it had, and the main reason for that had been Brenda's decision to prevent Privet making a getaway in the Land Rover, instead of joining in the fray. Now Privet was cornered in the house, and cornered animals were notoriously dangerous.

Walsh stood up and raised the megaphone. It was time to talk to Privet again and this time he'd put a little more sympathy and understanding into his voice. He might also mention that there was no death penalty in this country, and remind the man that there was still a case to be proved in a court of law.

He spoke persuasively, but again there was no reply. He shrugged and returned to the tractor shed, gratefully accepting a cup of thermos flask coffee.

The radio warned of the approach of the Chief Constable. Walsh went round the back of the tractor shed and down the lane to meet him. They walked together, out of the hearing of others.

'I'm not saying you haven't done well, but what the hell do you mean by setting yourself up in an ambush like that, Sidney. I don't pay you for your brawn and muscle, you know, it's your brains you should be using,' the CC said.

'With hindsight you might take that point of view, sir, but there was a risk to the life of the night-watchman. I needed to be on hand in case of developments and it didn't need an army at that stage, so I did the right thing, under the circumstances. Don't forget, we haven't got any positive proof yet that he did murder Trent and the girl, but now, if the worst comes to the worst, we can put him away for the attempted murder of the night-watchman.'

'You think you can talk your way out of anything, don't you?' the CC replied sharply. 'Well, what's the state of affairs now? Have you got any dialogue going yet?'

'No, not yet. I've been talking to him every twenty minutes, but he's not responded. Typical early-stage symptoms. We've tried the telephone as well, but he's just taken the receiver off. I'm almost a hundred per cent certain that he's on his own. I think we've just got to be patient,' Walsh replied, glad to be on safer ground.

'You seem to have got things well organized, but I've called in one of these siege psychology experts from London. I want us to be seen to be doing the right thing, even if he turns out to be useless.'

When the approaching dawn had lightened the eastern sky, Walsh drew his men back into positions that did not rely on darkness for their security, and carried on with the siege. He gradually became hoarse from using the megaphone, but the confidence of success in his voice remained unabated.

After six hours of frustration, of moving round the farmhouse from window to window, Privet finally faced up to the fact that escape from there was impossible, and accepted the inevitable with stubborn aggression. Suicide, as an option, did not merit any consideration in his mind. He packed a suitcase with the things he wanted with him, tossed the shotgun out of the window, and strode belligerently out from the front door.

21

Privet might have packed his suitcase in the expectation of being taken away, but if he had, he was mistaken. Instead he found himself back in his own small dining-room, where the sun's low-angled rays lit up slowly swirling dust motes and fell on his handcuffed wrists.

Confronting him were three tired police officers, whose strained faces were still smeared in places with sooty black.

'You can have a laywer here, if you like,' Walsh said, impatiently, for the third time.

For a whole half-hour Walsh had been asking questions and getting no answers. Privet's face had lost its expression of frustrated anger; but his jaw still jutted forward and his eyes still blazed with hostility.

'Why did you kill the young man?' Walsh demanded.

There was just a flicker of response in Privet's eyes, but that might have been a reaction to other noises in other rooms, of drawers being opened, cupboard doors being closed. Packstone's teams were methodically searching through the house.

'Sidney! You'd better come,' Packstone said from the doorway, his face stern and drawn.

Walsh heaved himself to his feet and followed him through the tiny hallway, into the kitchen.

'We've found the girl. She's in there,' Packstone said

grimly, pointing to the open door of a large walk-in pantry. Walsh peered in.

Originally it had been stone-floored; the slabs now leaned against the wall in a corner. A hole had been dug, deep and wide, and only partially refilled with hard core and rubble. Some of this had been cleared to one side to expose a pallid face and an arm. Just one body, but there was still plenty of room in the hole.

Walsh felt sickened as he turned away, content to leave Richard Packstone's men to complete the disinterment. He went back to confront Privet.

This time Walsh spoke softly, but in a voice that trembled with pent-up anger and menace, so much so that Privet's gaze rose from the table top before him, to Walsh's face, and his mouth opened a fraction in surprise.

'I didn't mean to kill the bastard,' he shouted angrily, smashing his clenched hands down on the table.

'Why, then?' Walsh demanded.

'He was starting to dig up there. I couldn't have that, but it was that spade that did it. I tried to get it off him and pulled, then all of a sudden he let go, the blade tore his throat open. I couldn't do anything about it, and that stupid girl was going mad, screaming and hitting at me,' Privet yelled viciously. 'She made me lose my temper, it was her own bloody fault.'

And that was all Privet would say. His mouth closed determinedly again and his eyes looked down at the table. After a few more minutes Walsh gave up.

'Get one of the uniformed sergeants to take him to headquarters, Reg. They can charge him with resisting a police officer, for the moment. We've got too many loose ends to tie up here. Brenda, I need a coffee and something to eat, as well as a wash. See what you can fix up.'

*

Walsh drained the coffee cup, took a sandwich from the plate and went outside into the farmyard. The sun was quite high now, and blazed warmly down from a clear blue sky in pleasant contrast to the cool gloom inside the house. A few flowers, pansies and marigolds, struggled to survive in the overgrown flower bed under the window.

On the other side of the yard was a heap of sand and gravel and a dirty cement mixer; unpleasant reminders of Privet's plan to conceal the evidence of murder under a thick layer of concrete.

He looked up at the house, that west-facing bedroom had a surprising view. It looked out over the trees that surrounded the farmhouse to a landscape of rolling fields and stumpy hedges, away to the distant horizon and the wood enclosing Barnhamwell Priory. The chair in the room and the binoculars were evidence that it had been used as a look-out. Walsh's watchers had been watched, yet by some trick of optics the existence of that view was not clear from the reverse direction.

A vehicle entered the yard, a Range Rover this time. Walsh recognized the passenger, he'd forgotten all about the college people and their treasure hunt.

'Chief Inspector! We were stopped at the top of the lane! Your men won't let us go up to the site, and we want to dig up the floor of the chapel this morning,' the Professor protested bluntly, looking with undisguised curiosity from Walsh's tired face to the other signs of activity.

'This is Dr Franklin, by the way, the archaeologist in charge,' he added, waving a podgy hand towards the driver.

'Good morning, Dr Franklin! Yes, I'm sorry, Professor, but we're a bit tied up with this Trent case this morning,' he replied, then turned to watch as a covered stretcher was carried out of the house and pushed into a waiting ambulance.

'Good gracious, that's not Privet, is it?' Professor Hughes exclaimed in surprise. 'Or is it the missing girl? Oh dear, good gracious me! Privet? But why? There's no motive, is there?' Hughes's face for once showed signs of bewilderment.

'There's always a motive, and we'll find his under the floor of your old chapel, if I'm not mistaken,' Walsh replied rather absent-mindedly, nodding in the general direction of the hill.

Packstone readily accepted Dr Franklin's offer of manual assistance.

'It's what we were planning to do this morning, anyway,' the Doctor explained, but 'we' obviously meant the tall, blond Nordic giant and a half-dozen other burly undergraduates, because Dr Franklin stood beside Hughes and the tall, lanky Packstone, as the heavy dark-grey stone flags were levered upright and carried away.

The sun now illuminated most of the area.

Walsh was only interested in the top half of the Chapel, that part to the eastern end which had been almost clear of turf and mosses, but he was content to watch until the whole floor was removed.

Packstone beckoned three of his assistants, and then set them to work scraping away the hard packed soil and rubble in the area Walsh had indicated. Dr Franklin walked over, produced a tiny, shining trowel from his pocket, and proceeded to kneel down and scratch carefully away, beside the other three. Finch joined him, carefully loosening the soil, and brushing it away with his left hand.

It was Finch who came to metal first. He sat back on his heels, nudged Franklin with his elbow, and pointed.

Together they cleared more. Flaky grey paint on rusty steel, some three or four inches beneath the surface. A spade was used to clear the rest of the earth, and another steel cupboard was revealed, beside the first, about fifteen inches wide and five feet long. The doors were uppermost and chromium-plated lever handles glinted silver in the sunlight. They resisted Packstone's attempts to turn them, so he picked up a spade to use as a lever, and heaved downwards. Something gave way with a jerk, the rusty hinges protested, but the door moved an inch or two.

Finch bent down, and wrenched it completely open.

Walsh walked over.

One glance was enough, a glimpse of white bone, of cloth. He went back to where Hughes was standing.

'But who are they?' Hughes asked, puzzled.

'Privet's wife, and the lover she was supposed to have run away with ten years ago, I imagine,' Walsh replied bluntly.

'You were right then, Chief,' Brenda said, with a grimace.

Hughes observed the tiredness and strain on both faces. 'Come and walk with me. I'd like you to tell me about it,' the Professor said, taking Brenda's arm, and moving towards the path out of the wood.

Walsh smiled reluctantly, but followed him.

'The locals probably knew Privet's wife was going off with another man before Privet did,' Walsh explained, 'so when she disappeared, it was only what they expected. She'd not made the kind of friends around here for her to keep in touch with, and had no family, apparently. Privet never reported her missing, he didn't need to. He just carried on and behaved just as everyone expected him to. With the fellow she was running off with, it was different.

When the chap's mother in Leicester hadn't heard anything from him after a few months, she got worried, and reported him missing at her local police station. She knew that he was going off with Mrs Privet, he'd told her that, and he'd told her that they were going abroad to Portugal, to make a new life out there. It happens like that, dozens of times each year. A few inquiries were made, where he worked and where he'd lodged after he'd sold his house. In both cases he'd left quite openly, saying he was going abroad, but leaving no forwarding address. There were no suspicious circumstances to warrant a more detailed investigation, so it became another file, another statistic. Nothing came out of the "Missing Persons" computer when we fed in the names of those concerned in this case. We had to read through each file area by area, until we found Mrs Privet's name mentioned,' Walsh told him.

'But you were specifically looking for a connection with Privet by then. Didn't he already have an alibi? What made you suspicious?' Hughes asked.

'Oh, he'd visited his old mother all right, as he did regularly, but he hadn't stayed there all that night like she said. She thought he always left early in the morning, before she woke up, but once she was in bed and asleep, Privet would head for home. It's easy to be confused if you're eighty-eight, you know. What made us suspicious? A silly thing, really. He hadn't shown up at the ruin at all, after Trent's killing. I didn't think anything of that at the time, but the other night, when the Satanists were here again, he didn't come then, either. Well, it's his farm, and a farmer ought to want to know what the hell's going on, on his land. It was enough to make me suspicious,' Walsh explained.

'So Privet must have somehow found out that his wife was going off with the other chap and waylaid them both.

I wonder why he buried them up here, of all places?' Hughes commented, rubbing his chin thoughtfully.

'He hasn't said yet, but I can hazard a guess. Privet was a regular church-goer, believe it or not. He probably killed in a mad fit of jealousy and hurt pride and then suffered remorse afterwards, that's often the case. This was once sanctified ground, so he probably buried them up here to try and alleviate his feeling of guilt. Here, where in the old days they used to have cock fights,' Walsh added, ironically, 'and he could keep the place under observation from the top window of his house. It's difficult to see from here, because wherever the light's from, it throws a shadow from those trees down there. That watching probably became a habit, too.'

'Ah!' Hughes interrupted. 'So he would have seen the Satanists' lights during their summer solstice ceremony.'

'And heard the cars as they arrived,' Walsh continued. 'He sneaked up to investigate. The Satanists wouldn't have worried him, but when they'd gone, Trent and the girl turned up with the metal detector and started digging right where he'd buried the bodies. That was a different matter. He says that Trent's death was an accident, and I suppose that's possible. Trent was drunk enough, earlier on that evening, to become aggressive with young Fry, so it's unlikely that he'd have submitted meekly when Privet tried to take his spade away. You've seen Privet, Professor. He's a strong man. You wouldn't give young Trent much of a chance in a fight with him, would you? Particularly if Privet lost his temper and panicked, which I think he must have done, because he didn't act very logically after that. He thought the Satanists would be blamed if he made Trent's death look sacrificial by putting that sharp flint in his hand, but that was foolish and he must have bitterly regretted it later on. If he'd taken the body away or even buried it carefully in the wood, he'd have stood a better chance of getting away with it.'

'Mrs Dubonis would have said that the Devil had taken over Privet's mind for his own purposes, Chief. In a way I suppose she would have been right,' Brenda suggested.

'Certainly evil was abroad in some form or other that night,' Walsh agreed, 'but having killed the boy by accident, let's say, I don't think he knew what to do with the girl and took her back to the farmhouse while he tried to work something out; but he couldn't, of course, not without giving himself away, so he had to kill her as well. Packstone thinks she was smothered with a pillow. I hope she was unconscious when he did it. Whether it was then that he decided to move the other two bodies from the ruins, I don't know. The floor in the pantry had certainly been dug out deep enough for all three, and that must have been done well before he learned that you wanted to excavate the site, Professor. Until then he'd seen our nightly patrols and he probably thought that all he had to do was wait, and eventually we'd give up. Your plans to start digging in earnest today meant that last night was his last chance to move those bodies before you found them. He tried, only we were waiting for him. So that's it, in a nutshell, Professor,' Walsh said, gazing away into the distance, across the bare stubble fields.

'That makes quite a story, Inspector, quite a story. Jealousy and fear, classical emotions combining into a saga worthy of the ancient bards,' the Professor added.

They had arrived back at the wood. In the ruins the work of removing the steel cabinets and their gruesome contents had been completed. Those who had been involved stood or sat about in the sunshine, resting after their labour and chattering amongst themselves, now that the cause of tension had gone.

They had left a deep hole, which extended on one side

up to the old chapel wall. Some of its coarsely mortared flints and large stones were laid bare, but there was also part of a smooth, dressed slab of limestone showing, eighteen inches or so deep, under a wider, darker stone only two inches thick. It reminded Walsh of part of a commemorative plaque, or foundation stone, and he said as much to Professor Hughes. The Professor nudged Dr Franklin's arm and pointed, excitement in his voice.

The Doctor looked, shrugged sceptically, but called two of his team and set them clearing away more of the rubble.

Packstone came back from supervising the removal of the two bodies and strode over to where Walsh and Brenda were standing. 'What's up now?' he asked.

'Treasure-hunting,' Brenda replied, with a slight smile.

It did not take the undergraduates long to expose the slab. It was nearly five feet long, and had been mortared into place under a dark granite lintel stone.

Walsh sat on the wall in the sunshine, content to watch, amused by Hughes's uncontrolled excitement.

Spades were used to lever the slab, gradually, from under the lintel, until it fell with a crash and split in two uneven halves on the hard rubble beneath.

Hughes waved his arms in glee. Exposed in the cavity, and almost completely filling it, was a powdery, greyish-white object; not a true cylinder, more of a box with very round edges. The ends were sharply square.

Hughes excitement spread, even to those who were unaware of the true reasons for it.

Dr Franklin shook his head in disbelief, inured by past diappointments against unwise optimism.

Packstone knelt down and scratched at it with a fingernail, tapped it with a knuckle, then scraped it with a trowel. 'It's lead, but it's in very poor condition, and it will certainly collapse if you try to lift it from both ends.

You'll need to ease it out very gently on to a prepared cradle, if you want to keep it intact,' he advised.

Hughes became serious all of a sudden, and tugged at Franklin's arm. He mumbled something about a laboratory and the need to have the means of preservation handy, before it was opened.

Franklin nodded, and snapped orders which sent his team running about. They constructed a stretcher with thick plywood in the middle, while Franklin went to fetch his Range Rover, driving it across the field, and backing it up as close to the wood as he could. The back doors were opened and the rear seats folded down, to make room for the strange cargo. They gradually eased the cylinder from its ancient resting place on to the cradle and carried it with tender concern to the waiting vehicle.

'Would you like to be there when we open it, Inspector?' Professor Hughes asked, before climbing into the passenger seat.

Walsh nodded.

'Bring your colleagues if they're interested. We'll do it in style later this afternoon. Come to my rooms about three, then. Bye for now.'

22

Hughes led them through into a lecture room near the laboratory. There were several tiers of wooden seating, rising by steps all around the central area, like a small version of a Roman amphitheatre.

Walsh noticed the presence of the young undergraduate Jeremy Fry, sitting near the front, and beside him was young Wendy. Walsh felt glad that Hughes had brought those two here; after all, they had started it all by finding the document in the first place. It looked as though young love might blossom into something strong, more permanent. The Barnhamwell site had been left in the charge of a uniformed sergeant, and Walsh had had time for a quick shower and a change of clothes. He felt refreshed and comfortable in sports coat and trousers. Brenda's face still looked a little pale, though, and there were dark shadows round Finch's eyes.

On the rostrum, the whitish lead cylinder lay in a wooden frame on a green-baize-covered table. Television cameras had been set up and a few spotlights, on tall black stands, had been switched on.

Another dozen dignitaries arrived, adding extra noise to the excited buzz of conversation from those already there. Hughes was out to make as much publicity out of the event as possible, or maybe there was inter-college prestige involved.

It was a bit risky, Walsh thought. Already he had overheard several comments suggesting that the container was only the lead lining of a mediaeval coffin.

Hughes returned, resplendent in red velvet waistcoat and maroon bow-tie, and stood on the rostrum. 'Welcome, ladies and gentlemen. As a result of the excavations organized by Downing College, with some assistance from King's, you see before you what we believe may well be a time capsule from the year eleven forty-two. The container will be opened by Dr Arthur Simonsly, of King's College. Thank you.' Hughes indicated a short, elderly, white-haired man, whose head had turned sharply on hearing Hughes's claim asserting Downing's dominant role in the finding of the lead container.

Walsh grinned to himself. Hughes would be a formidable opponent in the verbal battles for the final possession of those codices, if they did indeed exist. The moment of truth had arrived, however, and the audience held its breath in anticipation.

Dr Simonsly wasted no more time on ceremony. He picked up a small electric rotary saw, its blade no more than an inch in diameter, and carefully sliced off one end of the cylinder. Then he bent to peer inside.

He blinked in surprise, hesitated, then reached in with both hands. Dry fragments of cloth fell to the green baize but there was no mistaking the glint of gold as he raised high a magnificent chalice, studded with gemstones that flashed red, blue, green and silver in the bright lights.

The excited murmurs of his audience quietened as he reached in again. This time he withdrew a tarnished, bejewelled, silver reliquary. Next came a silver filigree cross, on a stepped plinth. Then, very carefully, he gradually eased out a thick bound book, greenish with age, about twelve inches by fourteen inches, and laid it gently on the table. He made no attempt to open it.

'Gentlemen! And ladies!' he added, as an afterthought. 'Much as I would like to, I shall not attempt to remove anything more. These books are plainly in a critically fragile state, and it is not for clumsy hands like mine to risk irreparable damage. Let us all be thankful for what we have seen, and leave the rest to those experts with the skill and knowledge to preserve these ancient codices, for the benefit of us all. Professor Hughes and Dr Franklin, you have both earned our deepest respect and gratitude for your determination and tenacity, in the face of persistent discouragement from many people, myself included. But our greatest thanks must go to Prior William and Brother Ignatius, of Barnhamwell, without whose foresight we would not be here now, with these treasures.'

Walsh thought the expression of utter happiness on Professor Hughes's face was one that would never, ever, be improved on. He hoped the cameras would preserve that for posterity, as well.